In The Cut

By

Arlene Brathwaite

BRATHWAITE PUBLISHING
www.brathwaitepublishing.com

Books by Arlene Brathwaite are published by

Brathwaite Publishing
P.O. Box 38205
Albany, New York 12203

Library of Congress Number:

ISBN – 10: 0-9797462-2-1
ISBN – 13: 978-0-9797462-2-2

This book was printed in the United States of America.

Acknowledgments

First and foremost I would like to thank God for making this possible. To all of the readers who purchased my books, and continue to show me love and support. I would also like to thank A & B Distributors in Brooklyn New York, Urban Knowledge Bookstores in Baltimore Maryland, Afrikan World Book Baltimore Maryland, Source of Knowledge Book Store Newark New Jersey, S & M Communications Albany New York, Seaburn Publishing Group/Black Book Plus Astoria New York, Rhonda Bogan of MochaReaders/James PR group for PR services, Kimberly Martin for book layout, Marion Designs for the hot book covers, Curtis Witters of Little Villa Publishing for all you do for me, know that I will never forget.

I would like to give a special thanks to my niece Timeka Dent for her continued support in letting North Carolina know what's really good. Dr. Funi Kasali MD for representing us as a people, I am so proud of your work. David Douglas, Denise Robinson, Tamicka Ramey, Sherodd Craft, Marshay Brathwaite, Akeama Foulks, Zanetta Motley, Arnita Norris, William Harris-White,

Patricia Harvey, Belinda Willingham, Curtis & Morticia Witters, Lenny Thomas, Adrienne White, Egypt Hill and Nicole Wise for spreading the word. There's no better advertisement than the word of mouth. Keep spreading the word y'all. My daughter Tamicka Ramey for proofreading. My husband Chris Brathwaite for copy editing and critiquing my work. Chris you are definitely my worst critic. To my family and friends who continue to be my backbone, and shoulders to cry on. Success is never achieved without people spewing hate from the sidelines. I will never understand why people are like that, but I drew the strength to deal with it from my husband's words of advice. "Don't worry about people when they talk about you. Only worry about them when they stop." Much thanks goes out to the sagacious advice of contemporary trail blazers Eric S. Gray, Anthony Whyte and to the dedicated readers of Urban Fiction who have come to expect nothing from me but the very best.

Chapter 1

In Rye, New York, Saint drove his BMW Z4 Coupe onto the property of a waterfront English Colonial home, framed by a collage of perennial gardens, sculpted shrubs, and shadowing Cypresses. The five-hundred-foot waterfront provided a breathtaking view of the Long Island Sound. It wasn't every day that he got a chance to rub elbows with the rich and powerful.

"There's no way you're going to convince me that black people live in this house," he said to his partner, Glenn.

"Black people don't live in this house," Glenn said, checking his face in the rearview mirror. "*Rich*, black people live in this house. So, don't be embarrassing me like you ain't got no sense."

Saint looked over at the two-piece orange, yellow, and pink suit Glenn had on and shook his head. "You don't have to worry about me embarrassing you. I think you got that covered."

"You won't be wearing that smirk on your face when you see Puffy wearing this outfit in his next video."

Glenn was a clothing designer who had an eye for fashion. After spending five years dressing mannequins in a Greenwich Village boutique, his big break came when the creative designer for Lane Bryant walked through the door and fell in love with one of his creations. She offered him a job with full benefits and two employees. A job he couldn't refuse. Within a matter of months, every wealthy plus-sized woman in the New York City area had his number on speed dial. Tonight was the unveiling of his *Beauty-full* clothing line.

"Is that Monique?" Saint asked, as a heavyset woman stepped out the back of a black stretch limo.

Glenn lowered his window as Saint pulled up alongside it. "Hey, girl, glad you could make it."

"Boy, please," Monique said. "I wouldn't miss your debut. It's all about you tonight."

Glenn got out and started chitchatting.

"Yo, Glenn, where am I supposed to park?"

Without missing a beat, the valet opened the car door. Saint stepped out and reached into his pocket. He pulled out a five-dollar bill and held it out to the valet.

"That won't be necessary, sir."

Catching Glenn glaring at him, Saint shrugged his shoulders and slid the bill back into his pocket.

"I'll see you inside," Monique said as she turned on her heels to leave.

"Yes, and I hope you enjoy the show," Glenn responded while backing up a few steps to talk to Saint. "This isn't The Tunnel or The Underground, so keep your money in your pocket."

"I was just trying to help dude out. Hell, he parks cars for a living."

"*Dude* makes more money in one month than you do in a whole year."

"Well, shit, see if you can hook me up with one of these valet gigs for the next show."

"Listen, when we get inside, you're going to be around some affluent people. So, try not to stare. They don't like when people stare at them, especially at a function that's supposed to be *private*," Glenn said, making quotation marks in the air with his fingers.

"Do I look like a groupie to you? I got better things to do in there than stare in people's mouths."

"Like what?"

"Like staring at them curvaceous, big-boned women in their lingerie and swimwear."

"You're such a man."

"And I better have a good seat this time. Last time, I was sitting so far in the back that all I could see was the back of everybody's head."

At the front door, a long-legged model named Gina, who would be their hostess for the evening, greeted Glenn and Saint. She led them through the estate and to the backyard. While Glenn was busy shaking hands and politicking, Saint walked toward the white pavilion that took up a good chunk of the yard. He quickly sized up the crowd and knew beyond a shadow of a doubt he was surrounded by money. He didn't know much about diamonds, but he knew the marble-sized diamond weighing down the finger of the lovely lady standing in front of him had to be worth at least twenty thousand. He stole a glance at the man by her side whispering something to her and immediately envied him. She was the type of sweet he would gladly rot his teeth on. Her spicy-brown complexion set off the silk floral-print dress she wore.

"Allow me to take you to your table," Gina said, using her cotton-soft hand to lead him by the hand.

Saint stared at her flowing hair lightly brushing against her back as she navigated through the crowd of the rich and powerful. The closer they got to the front, the more surprised Saint became. He was speechless when she stopped at a table only a few feet away from the stage.

"If there's *anything* you need, please don't hesitate to ask."

Not needing a moment to think, he blurted out, "I could use a drink."

"I'll be right back."

Saint watched as she sauntered off, wondering what she meant by *anything*.

Ten minutes later, Gina returned with a bottle of chilled Armand De Brignac, commonly dubbed as "Ace of Spades". Saint filled his champagne glass to the top, and as he chugged it down, he felt condemning stares from all around him. He glanced over his shoulder and saw the woman with the ridiculously big diamond ring avert her gaze. Although she was no longer staring at him, the traces of her grin let him know she found his uncouth act humorous. He picked up the bottle of champagne, stared at the spade embossment, and then remembered seeing it in Jay-Z's "Show Me What You Got" video.

Fuck'em. I'm not here to impress anyone, he thought, then refilled his glass and downed it in three swallows.

This time when he looked up, he noticed his long-legged hostess standing slightly to the side with a polite grin on her face.

"You're not going to just stand there all night, are you?" Saint asked, refilling his champagne glass for a third time.

She moved to sit down beside him, but he held his hand up. "Whoa! I didn't mean for you to sit down."

The last thing he needed was a woman sitting in his face while he tried focusing on the models parading up and down the runway half naked.

"I'm sorry," she said, evidently embarrassed. "I'll be right outside if you need anything else."

He gave her a thumbs-up, and with a smile, he dismissed her.

"Enjoying yourself already, I see," Glenn said, eyeing the bottle of champagne as he walked up to the table and sat down.

"I was thirsty."

"So you downed almost half a bottle of champagne?"

"I was really thirsty."

"How's the view?"

"This is what I'm talking about. This is how you're supposed to treat your boy. Front row seats, private table…"

"Glenn—" a woman's voice came from behind Saint.

Glenn stood up to greet her. "Olivia, how are you?"

Saint almost choked on his drink when the woman walked around him and came into view.

"I *was* doing just fine, if you know what I mean."

Just then, Glenn saw a man walking toward them. That's when he put two and two together.

"Hey, let me introduce you to a good friend of mine. Olivia, this is Clayton Andrews."

Saint hated when Glenn introduced him by his government name.

"And, Clayton, this is Olivia Martin."

"What's good?" Saint said.

"What's good?" Olivia repeated back, arching her eyebrow, and then she looked back at Glenn.

"I mean, how do you do, ma'am?" Saint told her, correcting himself to show more respect.

Before she had a chance to respond, Saint felt someone brush past him. Olivia sat down at the table and drank from his glass.

The man who had been approaching the table finally reached them. "Like I was saying, Olivia..." the man started.

"Byron, this is my husband, Clayton," Olivia said, interrupting him.

It was a good thing Byron didn't make eye contact with Saint, because Saint was just as surprised as him to hear those words come out of her mouth. The look on Saint's face would have easily let Byron know that Olivia was lying.

"Oh...I'm sorry." He looked at Saint and extended his hand out to him. "Byron Turner."

The two men shook hands.

"Clayton Andrews," Saint told him, playing along.

"Nice to meet you, Mr. Andrews. I didn't mean any harm by—"

Saint held up his hand, cutting him off. "Do me a favor, Byron, and get lost. The show's about to start."

Both Glenn and Olivia were stunned at Saint's bluntness. Without another word, Byron turned his glowing red face around, tucked his tail in between his legs, and walked off.

"If you don't mind," Saint said to Olivia, "I was drinking that."

She wiped the traces of her lipstick off the glass and slid it back to him. "I'm sorry. That was very rude of me."

Hearing his name being called, Glenn's head whipped around. Then he turned back to the two and told them, "I got to go. You children have fun. And, Olivia, make sure that's his last glass of champagne. He's driving."

"Hold up—"

Before Saint could get another word out, Glenn melted into the crowd. Saint looked back at Olivia. Each time he looked at her, she seemed to become more beautiful.

"So, Mrs. Andrews, when exactly did we get married? I must've been drunk out of my mind, because I don't remember any of it."

"Thank you for rolling with the story."

"Your real husband must go through hell every time y'all go out."

"Actually, I'm not married." She followed his eyes to the ring on her finger. "You'd figure this big-ass rock would repel every man on the planet."

"It seems like it's having the opposite effect. Why would you want to keep men off you if you're not married? I mean... you're beautiful and could have any man you want."

"I don't want a man. That's the whole point of me wearing this big-ass ring."

"Oh, I see. Men aren't your thing."

"What? Oh hell no! I *love* men. I'm just not looking to get into a relationship right now. Speaking of relationships, you and Glenn..."

"Glenn's my man." Saint spoke before he realized what she was really asking him. "Whoa, whoa! He's not my man as in *my man*. Glenn has his feminine ways, but he's not...and I'm *definitely* not gay. Why would you ask me something like that anyway? Do I look gay?"

"I was just making conversation."

"Well, change the subject."

"Okay, so what do you do for a living?"

"Next subject."

"Wow, that's a first. If I were to ask that question to the average man around here, I wouldn't be able to shut him up."

Saint took a swallow from his glass. "I'm not your average man, I guess." He ran his finger around the rim of his glass. "Let's just say I work with numbers."

"So you're an accountant or something?"

"Or something."

Olivia nodded as her eyes dropped to the Omega Speedmaster on his wrist. She then looked up at the light beard and moustache contouring his face.

"What is it that you do?" Saint asked, bracing himself for her answer. He didn't want to seem too impressed.

Olivia reached into her purse and retrieved her business card. Saint took it from her.

"Butta Cutz?" He read the back of the card, itemizing the services that her salon offered to men. "You're a barber?" he asked, looking back up at her.

"Yes."

"A barber, barber? As in you cut men's hair with clippers and what not?"

"Yes." Olivia could see him trying to conceal his smile. "You act like you've never heard of a female barber."

"To be honest with you, I haven't."

"Well, you're talking to one."

Saint looked down at the card. "You do manicures and pedicures, too?"

"Along with hot towel shaves and facials."

"And dudes…I mean, men actually come to your shop?"

"*You* need to come to my shop," she said, checking out his haircut.

"What? I just got my shit laced."

"You just got zeeked. You didn't pay for that, did you?"

"What's wrong with my taper?" he asked, looking into her eyes.

"That's what it's supposed to be? There's no blend. You can see the line going all around your head. Your points aren't sharp, and your hairline—"

"What about my hairline?"

"It's naturally crooked, so there's one of two ways of dealing with it. The right way, which is to make an imaginary line, or… like that," she said, pointing at his head. "Raising your points to square them off with the top of your hairline, which exposes more of your forehead."

"You trying to say I got a big forehead?"

Olivia shrugged her shoulders. "I'm saying your barber is whack."

Damn, Saint thought to himself. *She's sexy as hell, speaks her mind, cuts hair, and owns her own barbershop.* He tried handing back her business card, but she shook her head.

"Keep it."

He eyed her and couldn't help but smile. "So what brings you here?"

"One of my girls does some part-time modeling, so I came to support her."

"She's a barber, too?"

"Don't let her hear you call her that. She'll go ballistic. She's an Urban Hair Specialist."

"What's the difference?"

Before she had a chance to answer, the lights dimmed and a dark-skinned gentleman who appeared to be in his early fifties walked onto the stage and stood at the podium.

"Good evening, ladies and gentlemen. For those of you who don't know me, my name is Trevor Seeger, and I welcome you to my humble home for what promises to be the next hottest women's clothing line."

Everyone applauded.

"Please welcome a good friend of mine, Glenn Lemora."

Everyone stood and applauded. Saint felt happy for Glenn. He was finally living his dream. Glenn introduced the first model. Saint arched an eyebrow as the brick house of a woman walked out in a three-piece, black lace outfit. She had to be at least six feet, two hundred and twenty pounds, but she was cute and curvy as hell.

"That's my friend Grace," Olivia said as they sat back down.

Saint tried imagining Grace with a pair of clippers in her hand cutting hair. She walked to the end of the stage, strutting her stuff. She saw Olivia and winked at her. Then she gave Saint a curious glance before strutting back behind the stage as the next model walked out.

Over the next thirty minutes, plus-sized models of every color, shape, and size showcased Glenn's creations. Halfway through the show, Grace made her way to Saint and Olivia's table. She had on a powder blue pants and blouse ensemble.

"What's up, girlfriend?" She slapped Olivia high-five.

"You were hurting 'em, girl."

"I was, wasn't I?" Grace batted her eyes.

"You definitely did your thing up there," Saint said.

"Oh, I'm so sorry. Where are my manners?" Olivia said. "Grace, this is Clayton. Clayton, this is Grace."

"The pleasure's all mine," Saint said, shaking her hand.

"You's a cute fella and smooth. Don't be trying to talk to my friend. You see that big rock on her finger, right?"

"He knows about the ring, Grace."

"Damn, girl! Did you give him your social security number and bank account numbers, too?"

"We were just making conversation."

Grace looked Saint up and down. "You know how to fight?"

"Grace!" Olivia said, embarrassed.

"Why?" Saint asked.

"If you plan on getting with my girl, you better know how to fight because her brothers are overprotective."

"Brothers?" Saint asked.

"All four of them."

"It's not that kind of party," Olivia told her friend.

"I just figured I'd put the brother on point. Let's not forget what happened to the last one."

"The last one?" Saint asked.

"Okay, time for us to mingle," Olivia said as she stood up and grabbed Grace by the arm. "Nice to have met you. And thanks again for earlier with that creep."

"Not a problem. Take care of yourself. Hey, I might even stop by your barbershop."

"Barbershop? No he didn't just call your salon a barbershop." Grace said as Olivia pulled her away.

Saint watched as they disappeared into the crowd. He heard Glenn announcing that the swimsuit segment was next. He was so engrossed in Olivia's looks and personality that what he thought would be the highlight of his evening was nothing more than a blur of women walking back and forth. Olivia was a small woman, the type that would fit snug under his arm...petite, but not boyish. She had the body of a lean, but shapely gymnast.

For the rest of the night, he watched her work the crowd. She blushed, smiled, laughed, and her business cards seemed to magically find their way into the hands of those who stopped to talk to her. She reminded him of a woman in his past life. A fast talker, a shot caller.

I'm a tax-paying, working stiff, he said to himself. *I love my boring life. I…love my boring life.*

He finished the last of his champagne and admitted to himself that he hated his boring-ass life.

At the end of the show, Glenn closed out with a teary dedication to all those who believed in him and gave him the chance to showcase his gift to the world. As fate would have it, Saint and Glenn bumped into Olivia and Grace while waiting for the valets to bring their cars around.

"Thank you again for letting me model for you tonight," Grace said, hugging Glenn and kissing him on the cheek.

"The pleasure was all mine, girl. You brought out the sass in everything you put on."

Grace looked over at Saint. "You're a fashion designer, as well?"

"He's an accountant," Olivia said.

"He's a wh–" Glenn started to say.

Saint slapped him on the shoulder. "Yo, that show was definitely what was up."

"Yeah," Glenn said, rubbing his shoulder.

The valet pulled up Olivia's smoke grey Mercedes S-Class.

Saint stuck his chest out when the valet pulled his BMW Z4 alongside Olivia's ride.

"Nice wheels," she commented.

"It gets me from point A to point B," he replied humbly.

"Take care of yourself, Clayton." Olivia waved at him as she climbed into her car.

Saint waved at her as he got into his and pulled off.

"It gets me from point A to point B," Glenn said mockingly.

"So what's the deal with Miss Olivia?"

"She's a good girl, Saint."

"What's that supposed to mean?"

"Nothing. She's just not your type."

"And what's my type?"

"She's an honest girl."

"And your point?"

"My point is, it didn't take you more than five minutes before you lied to her. An accountant, Saint?"

"I told her that I work with numbers."

"You teach Math at the Adult Learning Center!"

"So you're saying she wouldn't be interested in a math teacher?"

"Not one who told her that he was an accountant."

"I never told her that I was an accountant."

"I didn't see you breaking your neck trying to correct her wrong assumption."

"I didn't see the need. Outside of these shows, we're never going to see each other."

"And what makes you so sure of that?"

"Like you said, she's not my type. She's honest and rich. The total opposite of me. I'm eating at McDonald's and Pizza Hut while she's having dinner at Justin's. If it wasn't for your fashion show, our paths would've never crossed."

"There was a time when you were eating at Justin's," Glenn stated with a smile.

"And that time will come again. You're about to be the next hottest thing, and like the good friend that I am, I'm going to be leeching off you."

"I owe all of this to you. If it wasn't for you, I would've never gotten this far."

"Remember that when the loot starts rolling in. And for the record, I *can* be honest."

"Yeah, and I got a goose that lays golden eggs."

Chapter 2

Olivia hadn't been open for business a hot twenty minutes before clients started filing in. Anyone who walked into Butta Cutz for the first time couldn't help but take notice of the cherry wood floors, exquisite oil paintings, and decorative beige and brown color schemes. Men from all walks of life, from drug dealers down the street to businessmen from Wall Street, would come to this little piece of heaven to get their minds right and heads tight. There were two large lounge areas. The one up front had a fifty-inch flat-screen HD TV mounted to the wall where the newest movie releases on DVD were shown. The male clients dubbed the lounge in the back "The Boardroom". It was where the "serious-minded" would get together and network. Shelves ran across The Boardroom's right side wall, replete with books ranging from self-help to urban fiction. There were also two computers in the far corner with internet access.

The first person you saw when you walked in was Miki, the receptionist. Miki was Japanese. She was born in Japan and raised in America. She was the type that could eat a cow and not gain an ounce of fat on her tight, tantalizing, hundred and twenty pound frame. This morning, she wore a pair of daisy dukes and a halter top. She had her waist-length hair styled in a tight bun.

"How's that coffee coming?" Olivia asked as she walked behind the reception desk and checked the appointment book.

"It should be done in a few minutes," Miki answered.

"Baby!" Olivia called out to her head manicurist.

"What up, Ma?" Baby was a sexy-ass tomboy. This morning, she managed to squeeze her 34-25-36 structure into a pair of her favorite overalls. The left suspender seemed to always hang off her shoulder, exposing part of her extra tight tank top.

"When the coffee's done, bring me a cup. I'll be in my office. You know how I get when I don't get my caffeine."

"I got you, Ma. Anything to keep you from cracking that whip."

Olivia walked into her office and played the messages on her answering machine. A few minutes later, Baby walked in with a cup of double espresso.

"Thank you, Baby. What would I do without you?"

"You'll be getting your own damn coffee."

"Hey, Olivia..." the last message on her machine started, "It's me, Byron Turner from the fashion show. The good-looking brother with the green eyes..."

"He clearly doesn't have low self esteem," Baby commented.

"Ill, how did he get my number?"

Byron's next sentence answered her question. "I didn't get a chance to get one of your business cards, but lucky for me, I was able to copy down your number from one you gave to a friend of mine at the show. Anyway, I was just wondering if we could hook up for lunch...strictly business, of course..."

Olivia looked like she wanted to vomit. "I think we can really take your men's salon to the next level. I'm talking having one in every major city. With my connections, we can't go wrong. Give me a call."

"He must not know you get men coming in here every day trying to sell you a dream so they can sample a piece of your pie."

"I swear, when I told him I was married, he started getting a hard-on right then and there."

"Well, you got nothing to worry about. If he shows his stalking-ass up in here, Jon-Jon and Mike are a phone call away. You know they ain't gonna let anything happen to their baby sis."

"If dude walks up in here, I'm going to roundhouse kick them green contacts out of his eyes."

"You go, girl. All the money you be spending on them kickboxing classes, you need to get your money's worth and start kicking some ass for real."

Olivia's intercom beeped; it was Miki. "Baby, if you're in there, your ten o'clock appointment is here."

"Sit him in my chair. I'll be right out," Baby said loud enough for Miki to hear.

Olivia took a long sip of her coffee, balled up her fist, and slammed it on the desk. "Damn! That's some strong-ass coffee, Baby. Just the way I like it. Remind me to give you a raise."

"I'm still reminding you about the raise you promised me three months ago."

"When I get around to giving it to you, remind me to double it."

"Yeah, I won't hold my breath on that one."

"Knock, knock," Grace said, peeking into Olivia's office.

"C'mon in, girl. Baby was just leaving."

"I'll kick it with you later," Baby said to Grace. "You know you got to let me know how the show went down."

"Girl…it went *down*. Olivia hooked up with a man."

Baby's mouth dropped open. "You mean to tell me that I was in this office for ten minutes and you didn't tell me you hooked up with someone?"

"I didn't hook up with anyone. You know how Grace exaggerates."

"She told him the truth about the rock on her finger," Grace said.

"Oh, hell no! I know Grace ain't exaggerating now. Gimme the rundown."

"Don't you have someone sitting in your chair waiting for you?" Olivia asked.

"That ain't nobody but Sam. He can wait."

"We don't keep our customers waiting. Take your ass out of here before I kick it. I've been dying to use my kickboxing in a real-life situation," Olivia said, smiling.

"I'll be back in an hour, and I want to know every single detail."

"GO!" Olivia said, crumpling up a piece of paper and throwing it at her. "You see what you started?" she told Grace.

"The girl is happy for you. I'm happy for you, and in about ten minutes, everybody in the salon is going to be happy for you."

"You think it'll take Baby that long to tell everybody my business?"

"You're right. Everybody probably knew the second she left the office."

"Which means Jon-Jon will be knocking on my door with the third degree."

"Tell your brother Jon-Jon that you're grown and can fuck whoever you want, whenever you want."

"Yeah, okay."

"What? You scared of him? What happened to all that Tae Bo, '*kicking ass for real*' shit you was just spitting?"

"Don't you have somebody's hair to cut?"

"I just came in to tell you that Glenn asked me to accompany him to a Black Tie event at the MGM Grand in Las Vegas."

"That's great."

"The top designers from all over the world are going to be there and of all the models. Glenn asked me to showcase one of his dresses. Do you know what that means?"

"That means you're on your way to a modeling career."

"No, silly. Do you know how much business Butta Cutz will get if we can get these guys to drop by and get a touch up or manicure?"

Olivia couldn't help but smile. This was the break Grace had been waiting for, and all she was concerned about was bringing in business.

"So you're coming, right?"

"Grace—"

"Grace, nothing. I'm not taking no for an answer. You think you got money pouring in now. Wait 'til the hood finds out who our new clientele is."

"How can I say no to you, Grace?"

"That's my girl."

"What's the square root of a hundred and forty-four, Mr. Reed?" Saint asked as he stood in front of the teenager's desk.

"All you have to do is think of a number that when you multiply it by itself it equals one hundred and forty-four."

"What the fuck do I need to know square roots for? This shit don't help me count my paper. This is some bullshit. Fuck a GED." Reed swiped his textbook off his desk and stood up.

Everyone in the class stopped what they were doing and watched him head toward the door.

"Hey, Reed!" Saint called after him. "You're right. Fuck a GED. A GED is nothing but a test you bust your ass studying for, and if you pass, all you get is a piece of paper. A piece of paper that doesn't guarantee you a job, success, or even a better life."

"Mr. Andrews, you must be psychic because you're reading my mind."

"No, Mr. Reed, I'm reading the script."

"What script?"

"The script that has been carefully laid out for you to follow. A script you know nothing about."

"You bugging, Mr. Andrews. There ain't no script."

"Oh, no?" Saint looked around the room as he spoke. "How many of y'all know someone who has not just one but two bachelor degrees and is working at Pathmark or some thrift shop at the mall?" He continued when he saw heads nod. "All those years of schooling, thousands of dollars they have to pay back in student loans, and what do they have to show for it? Where do you think they went wrong, Mr. Reed?"

"Not looking for a better job."

"They went wrong by *looking* for a job. From the time when we were in public school, we were taught to get good grades, graduate from high school, go to college, and then get a job. Right or wrong?"

"Yeah," Reed admitted.

"You bust your ass for close to sixteen years in school only to bust your ass for the next twenty-five years at a job that feeds you crumbs while the CEOs feast on cake. That's the script, if you were brought up that way. But, for the decision you're about to make by walking out of here, the script is drastically different. You walk out of here with the mindset that you're going to get your cake by any means necessary, whether by selling drugs, hustling people, or any other "get money" scheme you can come up with. However, it will only be a matter of time before you get knocked. And when you go to prison, guess what? The state gets thirty-five grand a year per inmate. How much of that do you think they're spending on an inmate? Either script you decide to follow, Mr. Reed, makes them no difference."

"And who's them?"

"The one percent that make billions a year from people like you who follow their script."

Reed looked at him for a moment and then cocked his head.

"So what script are you following, Mr. Andrews?"

"My own."

"Your own? You're working a blue-collar job making forty-five thousand a year, if that. What makes you so different from the motherfucker working at Pathmark?"

"What makes me different is...I *choose* to do this. Look around you," Saint said, spreading his arms wide. "This classroom is the last rung on the ladder. If you...and I'm talking to all of you...don't reverse the direction your lives are headed in, then your next step is a fall. A fall that many never come back from."

When Saint noticed Reed wasn't inching his way toward the door, he took that as a good sign.

"It's not about money for me. Trust me, this job doesn't pay nowhere near forty-five thousand a year."

"Then what is it about, Mr. Andrews?" a Spanish woman in her thirties asked.

"It's about me trying to make a difference. If I can get you to trash their script and write your own, one that improves the quality of your life and those in your circumference, then that's worth more than forty-five thousand dollars a year to me."

"And the only way you can show me how to do that is for me to get my GED?" Mr. Reed asked.

"A small price for what I'm offering."

Reed looked into the faces of the fifteen men, women, and teens mesmerized by the dialogue between him and Saint, and he could see the motivation Saint's words had given them. He slowly walked back to his desk and picked his GED book up from off the floor. With a huff, he sat down and opened up to the page he was last on.

In his peripheral, Saint saw someone standing at the entrance of his classroom. It was Glenn trying to get his attention. Saint addressed the class.

"I'll be back in a second. In the meantime, do questions thirteen through twenty."

"That was a deep spiel you gave in there," Glenn said when Saint accompanied him in the hallway. "Did you believe any of it?"

"They believed it, and that's all that matters."

Glenn shook his head. "The man with the golden tongue."

"Can you remind me why I'm out here in the hallway talking to you?"

"I need a favor."

"What else is new?"

"Friday night. MGM Grand in Las Vegas."

"I got plans."

"Plans?"

"Yeah. Friday night, in my bed, sleep."

"C'mon, Saint, don't do this to me. This is my biggest gig yet. Designers from Europe, France, Italy, you name it, are going to be there. I asked Grace to come along so she could show off one of my creations."

"You and Grace are going together. Why do I need to be there?"

"I need you to represent me."

"Represent you?"

"You could sell ice to an Eskimo. You speak French, Spanish, even German. What black man speaks German?"

"Glenn—"

"Olivia's going to be there."

"And? She's out of my league, remember?"

"I'm just saying. She'll be there to keep you company in case you get bored."

Saint looked him up and down, then shook his head. "I'll do this on one condition," he said, holding up his finger.

"Anything."

"For as long as you live, don't *ever, ever* come to my job wearing orange spandex again."

Saint's apartment was a simple one-bedroom pad, scarcely furnished and with nothing in plain view linking to his past. He leaned against his dresser staring at the cotton/silk single-breasted tux laid out on his bed for the next night's exclusive event in Las Vegas.

"I can be honest," he said out loud, remembering what Glenn said to him while they were on their way home from the last show. "The only reason why I'm going to this snobby event is to see Olivia again. There, I said it. I'm feeling homegirl, and I want to see her again."

He broke out in laughter. It felt so good to feel emotions for another human being again. The last woman he had been intimate with nearly killed him. He fingered the stab wound on his chest. He knew Olivia was nothing like *her*.

"Holla at your boy!" Jon-Jon barked as he walked into Butta Cutz. He licked his lips while approaching the reception desk.

"What up, Miki?"

"How you doing, Jon-Jon?"

"Better…much better," he said, eyeing her long legs. "How's business?"

"It's business as usual."

"No doubt. Is my sister in her office?"

"Yeah."

"I'ma go holla at her. I'll be back to holla at you later, though." Jon-Jon winked at her as he headed toward the back.

Miki's smile vanished as soon as he did.

Jon-Jon knocked on Olivia's door and entered. "What's cracka-lacking, sis?"

"Jon-Jon, how many times do I have to tell you to stop barging in on me like that?"

"Save that shit for them hoes. I'm family, and we ain't got no secrets."

"It's not about secrets; it's about respect for each other's privacy."

"I ain't come here to hear all that. Check it, right. I need a favor. I'm seeing this girl–"

"And?"

"And she attends Hunter College."

"Really?" Olivia said, surprised.

"Yeah, I'm stepping my game up."

"When you gonna step your wardrobe up and rock something else other than baggy pants, hoodies, and fitteds?"

"Step up to what? Tight-ass suits and pointy shoes? Forget about how I dress. Back to my girl. She needs a job."

"Bring her in for an interview."

"Interview? She's looking for a job, not an interview."

"I don't know her, Jon-Jon. I got to at least meet her before deciding whether or not to give her a job."

"You know me, and I'm vouching for her. That's good enough."

"Like I said, bring her in for an interview, and I'll see what I can do."

"You on some bullshit, Olivia, word."

"Why I got to be on some bullshit, Jon-Jon? I'm running a legitimate business."

"A business your *brothers* help hold down."

"Don't even go there."

"All I'm saying is I don't ask for much, and when I do, I got to jump through hoops 'n shit."

Olivia closed her eyes and took a deep breath. "Listen, bring her in Monday morning just so I can go through the motions. My employees will flip if I just hire someone without running it by them first."

"So you're going to give her the job?"

"Yes, Jon-Jon, I'm going to give her the job. Just make sure she comes in Monday morning."

"I knew I could count on you, sis." Jon-Jon pulled up a chair and kicked his feet up on her desk. "So what's this I'm hearing about you fucking with some nerd-ass accountant?"

Olivia opened her desk drawer and grabbed the bottle of aspirin.

Chapter 3

Saint and Glenn arrived at J.F.K. Airport just before noon. Mr. Seeger greeted them with a brisk handshake and a wide smile.

"The ladies are already onboard," he said, referring to Grace and Olivia.

When Glenn told Saint earlier that Mr. Seeger was flying them to Las Vegas in his private jet, he was impressed.

The runway was an eardrum's nightmare. Everything from the roaring of jet engines to the click-clacking of baggage carts being towed to luggage conveyor belts hit Saint from all sides. He winked at Glenn as they followed Mr. Seeger up the grip-textured aluminum steps of the Gulfstream VI. As the cabin door closed behind them, it felt like they entered a soundproof booth. The interior was red with gold trimming. The red leather seats were club-sized and looked inviting. Some faced each other with a table bolted down in between them. Saint's eyes lit up when he saw Olivia. She gave him a head nod and a smile. Grace, on the other hand, ran down the aisle and gave Glenn a hug and a wet kiss on the cheek.

"You don't know how much this means to me, Glenn. Thank you so much."

"No, thank you," Glenn said, kissing her hands.

"Hi, Clayton," Grace said, giving Saint a hug.

"Hi, Grace. Good to see y'all again." Saint cut his eyes at Olivia, who was wearing a plain sweatsuit. She wasn't wearing any makeup, but she still looked sexy as hell.

He hung up his garment bag containing his tux on the overhead hook next to Grace and Olivia's garment bags and followed Glenn and Grace down the aisle. He sat in the seat opposite Olivia and reached over the table to shake her hand. He smiled when he saw the sparkling diamond.

"So are we going as husband and wife tonight or…?"

"I think I can keep a couple fashion designers at bay, but just in case, be ready to call me darling or sweetheart," she responded with a wink.

Mr. Seeger picked up a phone that was linked to the cockpit. He shook his head and grunted a few words before letting his guests in on the conversation.

"We're about to take off, so the pilot wants us to buckle up. We should be in Las Vegas in about five hours. If you'll excuse me, I have to make a couple calls."

"Thank you once again, Mr. Seeger," Glenn said.

"My pleasure. Anything for the future icon of fashion." With a nod, Mr. Seeger headed toward the front of the jet.

"Seems like he has a lot riding on you, Mr. Future Icon of Fashion," Saint said.

"A lot of people do. That's why I have to hit it off big with these guys tonight. So what should we be expecting?" Glenn asked Saint in a stressed tone.

"The same thing you see at all these functions. Eccentric men with deep pockets and exotic women wrapped around their necks like scarves. You're new to the game, so they're going to try and dazzle you with a little glitter and a lot of bullshit." Saint looked over at Grace and Olivia. "Excuse my choice of words, but I got to call it what it is."

"Keep it real, nigga," Grace said.

Olivia swatted her on the shoulder. "What did I tell you about using the N word?"

Saint continued. "The most important thing to remember, Glenn, is don't sell yourself short. You're a damn good fashion designer, and you got a dimepiece on your side."

Grace blushed.

"They're going to love your creativity," Saint added. "I can guarantee you that."

"And how do you know so much about these guys, Mr. Accountant?" Olivia asked, leaning over the table toward him.

"In my line of work, I meet all kinds of people. Some I can't stand the sight of and others…I can't stop looking at. So, remember what I said, Glenn, and–"

Olivia blinked. *Oh, you're good. I didn't even see that one coming. Some I can't stand the sight of and others I can't stop looking at.*

She grabbed her bottled water out of the cup holder and took a few swallows to extinguish the heat of the blush spreading across her face. He was different. He wasn't the shallow type she was accustomed to dealing with. If they weren't flashing their jewels, they were patting the knot of money in their front pocket. Olivia didn't consider herself rich, but she was well off.

Her wealth was her gift and her curse. She was blessed to be able to take care of her brothers and those who worked for her, but the one thing that money couldn't buy her was the ability to look into the hearts of the men who wanted to get with her. Did they want her money or did they just want a quick lay? Either way, she had no true way of knowing, and the line of defense that her brothers provided between her and the male population kept out a lot of creeps. However, it also kept out a lot of good men. From what she could sense, Clayton was smooth, but he wasn't game-tight. Cocky, but not arrogant.

"So how did you two guys meet?" Grace asked. "He's a fashion designer and you're an accountant. You two are from two different worlds so to speak."

"It's a long story," Saint said, hoping she'd get the hint.

"Well, can you tell it in five hours?"

Saint looked at Olivia and could tell she was just as curious. When he looked over at Glenn, he had the "let's-see-if-you-can-tell-the-truth" grin on his face.

"Well...we met in Paris." Saint gave Glenn the "yeah-I-told-the-truth" look.

"Paris?" Grace said, surprised.

"Yeah. Glenn was studying fashion design under the tutelage of a Rumanian tailor named Petrescu. I was Petrescu's...number man at the time. About three months down the line, Glenn's parents found out he had dropped out of college to pursue his fashion dreams. They immediately cancelled his credit cards and stopped putting money in his bank account. When Petrescu offered to take an alternative form of payment, Glenn punched him in the face, packed his things, and behold, the future 'icon of fashion' was knocking on my door at ten o'clock at night.

He promised if I let him stay the night, he would be out of my life in the morning. That was five years ago."

"Wow, and now y'all are the best of friends."

"Actually, Glenn is my only friend."

"Aw, poor baby," Grace said, pinching his cheek. "I'll be your friend, and Olivia will be your friend, too. Right, Olivia?"

"Sure."

"Well," Grace said, exhaling, "being that we got all that out the way. Did my ears deceive me the other night or did you call my girl's salon a barbershop?"

When Seeger's jet landed, there was a Maybach 62 waiting for them.

"Niiice," Grace said, elbowing Olivia.

At the MGM Grand, they were greeted by a personal butler who showed Grace and Olivia to their suites, and then Glenn and Saint to theirs.

"We're on top of the world," Glenn said, staring at the floor-to-ceiling windows of the two-story suite of the recently opened sky lofts that were on the two top floors of the MGM Grand.

"Not yet, Grasshopper," Saint said, patting him on the shoulder. "Remember what I said about the glitter and bullshit."

"Speaking of which, I'm impressed. You actually told the truth about how we met."

"I told you I could."

"Of course you left out the part about Petrescu being part of the Rumanian mafia and that sexy assassin that put a six-inch knife through your chest."

"I didn't want to bore them with details."

"So when are you going to tell Olivia that you're not an accountant? I peeped the way you were looking at her. You're feeling her."

"Since when did you become a master at reading people?"

"I ain't got to be a master to see the sparkle in your eye when you first saw her on the plane."

"Stop worrying about me and start thinking about how you're going to get in Grace's panties. That *is* one of the main reasons you asked her to come, right?"

"Any suggestions?"

"Just one. Be honest."

Glenn and Saint met Grace and Olivia at their suite and accompanied them to one of the hotel's private lounges where they were introduced to fashion designers who didn't need any introduction. Both Glenn and Saint were wearing tuxedos. Olivia wore a strapless gown and a diamond necklace. Grace was the breathtaker. She had on a hand-fluted, silk matte jersey gown that cuddled her.

"You were right," Olivia said, whispering in Saint's ear.

"About what?"

She pointed with her chin to the man with three gorgeous women surrounding him. "Like scarves, right?"

He nodded.

"I'll be right back," she said, about to mingle.

Saint grabbed her by the elbow. "Please don't tell me you're going to do what I think you're going to do."

"What's that?"

He looked down at her clutch purse. "How many business cards do you have in there?"

"Ten, maybe fifteen."

Saint gave her the look.

"Fifty, but I don't plan on giving them all out."

"You're not going to give any out."

"And why's that?"

"Look around you, Olivia. What do you see?"

"Fashion designers, women, waiters..."

"Look past the obvious."

"I give up. What am I supposed to be seeing?"

"Business cards."

Olivia squinted her eyes at him.

"The dresses, the gowns, the suits, the tuxedos, the jewelry, the eyewear, and even some of the women are all for sale. This gathering is nothing but a commercial whose actors are also the consumers. This is how *they* advertise. You go pulling out business cards and start handing them out, they're liable to call security and have you thrown out into the street for vulgarity."

"Oh really?" Olivia didn't look convinced.

"Really. If you don't believe me, go ahead." He released her elbow.

Olivia bit her bottom lip as she looked around the room. "So how am I supposed to let them know about Butta Cutz?"

"First of all, they're going to need a damn good incentive to want to come to Butta Cutz. And the only incentive that works on these folks is money."

"Money? I'm not going to pay them to come to my salon. That's defeating the purpose."

Saint shrugged. "Of course there's another way."

"And what's that?" she asked, tensing her shoulders.

"Pay them, but pay them with their own money."

"Huh?"

"Saint!" the 55-year-old Rumanian called out as if he had seen a ghost.

It took Olivia a few seconds to realize he was referring to Clayton, and it took her a few more seconds to realize he was speaking to him in French.

Saint bowed his head and then replied to what the Rumanian had asked him. Olivia was amazed at how Saint's voice took on a French accent, speaking the language as if it was his native tongue. He gestured toward Olivia and continued his conversation with the Rumanian.

"Olivia, this is Mr. Petrescu."

Olivia remembered the name from their conversation on the jet.

Mr. Petrescu grabbed Olivia's extended hand and kissed it.

"It is a pleasure to meet you." He spoke English this time, but Olivia still had trouble understanding him through his thick accent.

"It is a pleasure to meet you, as well, Mr. Petrescu."

"Please, call me Laurent."

"Okay, Laurent."

"You've gained weight, my friend," Petrescu said to Saint.

"I'm not as active as I used to be."

"So I've heard," Petrescu said, grinning at the double meaning of Saint's words. "So what brings you here, business or pleasure?" Petrescu asked suspiciously.

"Neither. I'm just accompanying a friend," Saint replied, pointing with his chin in Glenn's direction.

Petrescu looked over and then slapped his hands on his cheeks. "He still looks magnificent. I hear he's becoming famous here in America."

"He's the future icon of the fashion industry, Laurent."

Petrescu laughed, but the bite in his stare told Saint that he hadn't forgotten the night when Glenn punched him in the face. He wasn't mad at the fact that Glenn punched him. He was outraged that Glenn didn't accept his intimate proposal. After all, he was Laurent Petrescu. No one said no to him.

He bowed his head to Olivia. "I will leave you two to mingle while I go and pay my respects to Glenn."

Before departing, he locked eyes with Saint. The only word Olivia understood in Petrescu's parting words in French was a name: Josephine.

They both watched Petrescu as he approached Glenn and hugged him like a long lost relative. Olivia and Saint both smiled at the way Glenn greeted him with a cardboard hug and a plastic smile.

Olivia stepped back from Saint and looked him up and down.

"You're full of surprises. You speak French?"

"I speak it a little."

"A little?"

"I lived in Paris for a few years. I was forced to learn the language to get around."

"Whatever you say, *Saint.*"

"That's my nickname. Correction, that *was* my nickname."

"And who's Josephine?" Olivia peeped the way he stiffened. "I'm sorry. I shouldn't have asked you that. It's none of my business."

"Clayton!" Glenn called out, waving him and Olivia over.

As they walked toward Glenn and Grace, Saint could see he was sweating and nervous as hell.

"I would like you to meet Marion Claude."

"Marion Claude? That name sounds so familiar," Saint said. Then he snapped his fingers. "I read an article on you in *Fortune 500*."

Marion nodded humbly. "Pleased to meet you, Mr.–"

"Andrews. Clayton Andrews." Saint extended his hand. "And this lovely lady is Olivia Martin."

"A pleasure," Marion said, kissing Olivia's hand.

"I see you've bumped into an old friend," Saint said to Glenn as he looked toward Petrescu, who was standing next to Glenn.

"Yes, Laurent and I have some catching up to do," Glenn said, moving closer to Grace.

"Please, if you will," Marion Claude said, motioning for them to sit at his table.

"Your friend Glenn speaks highly of you, Mr. Andrews."

"What are friends for, right?"

"I offered to buy this beautiful masterpiece," he said, gazing at the dress Grace was wearing, "as a present to take back to France for my wife, but he insists on you handling all of his business transactions. Name your price."

"We have all night, Mr. Claude. I'm sure we can find a time when we can talk with less people around," Saint told him.

"This is the perfect place. We're amongst friends, no?"

Saint said something in French that brought a smile from Laurent Petrescu, a smile from Marion Claude, and a stunned look from Grace, who just found out that Saint spoke French.

He translated for Glenn, Grace, and Olivia's benefit. "Friends and money is the recipe for disaster."

"I like that saying. It's sooo true," Marion said, clasping his hands together. "Now tell me your price for the dress."

Saint looked into Glenn's big brown eyes and could see he was desperate enough to rip the dress off of Grace's back and give it to Marion Claude for free.

"Ten thousand."

"What!?!" Claude and Petrescu said at the same time.

Glenn looked like he wanted to cry.

"What!?!" Saint mimicked. "What as you didn't hear me, or what as in you can't afford it?"

"I assure you, Mr. Andrews, money isn't an issue," Marion Claude said, sticking his chest out slightly.

"So then, it's settled. Ten thousand dollars…cash."

"Mr. Andrews—" Marion started.

"Mr. Andrews, what?" Saint said, now speaking in French. "You know as well as I do that Glenn Lemora is about to be the next big thing in fashion. In six months, that dress is going to be worth triple the price we're asking for tonight. And for the record, you said you want to purchase the dress for your wife, but the article in *Fortune 500* said you were a bachelor. Was that a misprint?"

Marion Claude busted out laughing, and like a chain reaction, Petrescu and the women clinging onto Marion Claude laughed like obedient lackeys.

"I see why Mr. Lemora allows you to handle his affairs," Marion responded in French.

"Game recognizes game," Saint replied with a wink.

Marion spoke in English. "Out of respect for Mr. Glenn Lemora, it will be my pleasure to buy one of his originals. Unfortunately, I can't get my hands on ten thousand dollars cash, but if you're willing to take six now, and—"

Saint sat back and put his arm around Olivia. "Mr. Claude, did I mention that Miss Martin owns a men's salon and that she is a professional barber?"

"Really?"

"Yes."

"And where is this salon located?"

"Downtown, Manhattan…the center of attention."

Marion Claude arched an eyebrow.

"I tell you what. Arrange to have the six thousand sent to Mr. Lemora's room—"

"And what of the four thousand?"

"Four thousand should about cover your traveling expenses to New York, yes?"

"So let me get this straight. You will give me the dress and write off the four thousand as traveling expenses if I agree to visit Miss Martin's…salon?"

"Exactly, and bring your entourage with you."

Olivia was smiling on the inside. What Saint said earlier began to make sense. Use their money to pay them to come.

Marion Claude stared at Saint, contemplating his proposal.

"Just imagine the publicity this would attract. News reporters from every newspaper, T.V. station, and radio station will be there."

"And how would they know I would be coming?"

"You know you can never keep the lid on something this big. Someone is bound to talk."

"And you're sure about that?"

"Bet my life on it."

Marion Claude nodded.

"What day would be good for you?" Saint asked.

"I must be back in France no later than Wednesday. Is Monday good?"

Saint looked at Olivia.

"Yes," she said, slowly recovering from awe. "Monday is perfect. How many people should we be expecting?"

Marion Claude opened his arms in a wide arching motion, causing Olivia to look around. "Everyone who is here will be there."

"You scare me," Olivia commented, as she and Saint stood out on the balcony savoring the night's cool breeze.

"Okay…I didn't see that one coming," Saint said, taking a swallow from his wine glass.

"The way you hustled Marion Claude—"

"I didn't hustle him. I did him a favor."

"Oh really? How's that?"

"He craves the spotlight. So, I shined a gigantic one right in his eyes."

"Blinded him with the light while you took off with his loot like a thief in the night."

"You've learned well, Grasshopper."

Olivia laughed. She locked eyes with him as he inched closer to her and ran his hand along her arm.

"Clayton—"

"Shhh." His fingertips sent tingles through the back of her hand. He wrapped his hand around her wine glass. "Two glasses of wine are more than enough. Anything more will have you holding your head in the morning."

He took the glass from her and turned to set it on the balcony's table.

Olivia exhaled, realizing she'd stopped breathing. She folded her arms, embarrassed that she'd braced herself for him to kiss her.

"You okay?" he asked, turning back to her.

"I'm fine."

"Are you cold? We can go back inside."

"No, I'm fine."

"So you like?" he said, pointing to his fresh haircut. "I had my barber do that imaginary line thing-a-ma-jig, and he blended the taper."

"It's all right."

"You didn't even give it a good look-over."

"I'm a barber, remember? I checked your do out the second you got on the plane."

"You said it's all right, meaning?"

"Meaning, you need to go to a barber who knows what they're doing."

"A barber like you."

"You'll never find a barber like me."

"Oh, do I sense a little grandiosity in that statement?"

"I call it like it is."

"So, be brutally honest. What's wrong with my do?"

Olivia slowly began walking around him.

"Don't move," she said when he started to turn his head.

She walked a full circle and then stopped directly in front of him. She slowly ran her fingers through his hair. She then tilted his head down.

"Hmm."

"Hmm, what?" he asked.

"You got some Indian or Spanish in you."

"My mother's Spanish."

"That explains the curly hair and your olive brown complexion. Your haircut looks good…to the untrained eye, but I would've done two things differently."

"What's that?"

"Parts of your hair are uneven. That's because your barber doesn't use scissors to even you out. With soft, curly hair like yours, you'll never get it even with just clippers."

"And the second thing?"

"I wouldn't take too much off the top. You're thinning up there."

"What?" Saint jumped back and patted the top of his head. Olivia started laughing.

"You're fucking with me, right?"

"No, I'm not messing with you."

"You don't curse, do you?"

"Why do you say that?"

"On the plane when Grace used the N word, you immediately checked her on that. Just now, I asked if you were fucking with me, and the natural response would be, 'No, I'm not fucking with you', but you said, 'No, I'm not *messing* with you'."

"No, *Saint*, I don't curse."

"But you used to, right?"

"What's up with the *Date Line*, Barbara Walters interview?"

"Just trying to get to know you."

"I should be the one asking the questions, Mr. Saint, the French hustler. So do you speak any other languages?"

"Umm, let's see…I speak a little Italian, Spanish, Swahili, and German–"

"Swahili?"

"Just a little."

"And German?"

"It's a long story."

"Is any story with you ever short?"

He raised his wine glass to his lips. Olivia stopped him and took it from him.

"Don't want you waking up in the morning holding your head."

"So, tell me. How did a beautiful woman like you become a barber?"

"It's a long story."

"That's my line."

"I didn't know you owned exclusive rights to it."

"So how did this career come to be?"

"Well, as Grace told you at the fashion show, I have four brothers: three older than me and one three years younger than me. Jon-Jon, my younger brother, received a pair of clippers as a present for his thirteenth birthday. The next morning, he had me in the bathroom trying to cut his hair. We were in there for hours. I would be doing good, and then, I would slip or blink and—"

"You'd zeek him."

"Basically. A couple months later, I was lacing him up so good that my other brothers let me do their heads. Then Jon-Jon, being the visionary he is, started bringing his friends over to get their heads done. Pretty soon, our basement became the unofficial neighborhood barbershop."

"So you were getting paid."

"Yeah, right! Jon-Jon was charging those dudes fifteen dollars apiece. I was lucky if he gave me five dollars out of the fifteen."

"That sucks."

"That's why I told him to go f— himself, and I went to ol' man Brady who owned the official neighborhood barbershop.

He'd already heard of my skills, so he immediately put me to work and sent me to barber school to make me legit. I was nineteen at the time."

"That was nice of him."

"In his eyes, I was the daughter he never had. Five years later, he died. That's when I knew how deep his love was for me. He left me everything."

"Seriously?"

"The barbershop and the apartments above the barbershop that I didn't even know he owned."

"So you owned a barbershop and apartments at the age of twenty-five?"

"Yep. So, you can imagine the drama. Local businessmen trying to buy me out, the wannabe thugs trying to use my establishment to do their dirt, getting proposed to at least once a week. Luckily, my brothers had my back. The hood respected them and my competition feared them. Back then, Butta Cutz was just a fantasy I had. It took me six years to save up the money, but I did it. I gave Brady's barbershop a facelift and made it more than just a barbershop. And here I am three years later, the proud owner of Butta Cutz." Olivia walked to one of the cushioned chairs, sat down, and took off one of her shoes. "I hate high heels."

Saint pulled a chair in front of her and patted his lap. "C'mon, put it up here."

Olivia looked around and then put her foot on his lap. Saint's fingers immediately went to work, dissolving the soreness in the arch of her foot. Olivia melted back into the chair and a sigh escaped her lips. Saint then used both his thumbs to massage the pressure points in the sole of her foot.

"Oh God! That feels so good."

Saint looked down at her other foot and smiled when he saw how quickly she came out of her other shoe. He worked his thumbs in between her toes, causing Olivia to close her eyes. She put her other foot on his lap.

"You're not falling asleep on me, are you?" he asked as he began massaging her other foot.

"No, I'm just enjoying the moment. How much do you charge? I'm about to give you a job."

They both laughed.

"So, Clayton, being that I told you my whole life story, what about you?"

"Well—"

"Let me guess. It's a long story?"

"Actually, it's not."

"Whoa, you *are* full of surprises."

"Let's see. Both my parents died when I was two. A friend of the family adopted me. Every summer, I would be shipped away to a different country, which is how I learned how to speak so many different languages."

"Schooling?"

"Private tutor."

"Any kids?"

"No."

"Significant other?"

"Never."

"Someone you used to like?"

Saint's mind flashed to *HER*. "I wouldn't say liked. I would say I was pussy whipped."

Olivia's eyes popped open.

"I call it like it is."

"Okay. I just wasn't prepared. Most men don't admit to being...whipped."

"I said pussy whipped."

"I know what you said."

"So, you've ever been...whipped?"

"Honestly?"

"Please."

"No, but I was infatuated with this guy once."

"What happened?"

"We had an argument one night. Things got hairy. He hit me, told me I was his bitch, and that I better stay in my place. He even dared me to tell my brothers."

"And you told them?"

"Heck no. I fucked him to sleep. Then I bashed his head in with a cast-iron frying pan."

"You cursed."

"You're a bad influence on me."

"So you bashed him in the head with a frying pan."

Olivia started laughing. "Oh God, it was so funny. I hit him and he sat straight up. Scared the crap out of me. The second hit put him out and left a knot on his head the size of a bowling ball."

They both started laughing.

"There you are!" Glenn said, walking out onto the balcony with Grace right behind him. "We were looking all over for you."

"Y'all weren't doing anything freaky, right?" Grace asked.

Olivia jerked her feet off of Saint's lap and slipped them into her shoes. "I got two words for you, Grace," Olivia said, holding up two fingers. "Tae Bo."

"I got the chauffeur bringing the Maybach around so we can go for a ride and celebrate," Glenn said.

Saint folded his hands together. "Celebrate what?"

"Six thousand dollars…in cash. You're the man!"

"That was smooth, Clayton," Grace said. "Shoot, for six thousand cash, I would've given him the dress and a little freak peek. You know what I mean?"

"Grace!" Olivia said, getting out of the chair.

"Shoot, for six thousand cash, I would've given him a freak peek, too," Glenn said, giving Grace a high-five.

"You two are sick," Olivia said.

"Mr. Andrews?" A waiter walked out onto the balcony with a cell phone on a platter. "You have a call, sir."

"A call for me?"

"Yes, sir."

Saint picked up the phone. "Hello."

"My beloved, Saint. Oh, how I missed hearing your voice."

Saint almost swallowed his tongue.

Chapter 4

"Are you okay?" Olivia asked Clayton.

Saint cleared his throat. "Yes. I really have to take this call. Why don't y'all go ahead without me?"

"We'll wait for you," Grace said.

"No, really. Y'all should go." Saint gave Glenn the look.

This time, Glenn almost swallowed *his* tongue. "C'mon, y'all," he said, grabbing Grace and Olivia by their hands. "He's going to be awhile with that call."

Olivia didn't move.

"Please, Olivia," Saint said. "It's business. I have to go to the suite, boot up my laptop—"

"Okay. I guess we'll see you in the morning," Olivia said, allowing Glenn to usher her off the balcony.

"Yes, tomorrow," Saint replied with a smile. When they were out of hearing distance, he took a deep breath and then spoke into the phone. "How did you know I was here?"

"My love, I know where you are twenty-four hours of the day, seven days of the week. What I don't know is why you are in Las Vegas."

"Josephine, it's a get-together for a bunch of clothing designers."

"I know what it is. What are *you* doing there?"

"I'm having a few drinks with friends."

"And you have no idea what's happening at that get-together?"

"When I saw Petrescu, I knew it was serving a dual purpose. And I don't want to know what the other purpose is."

"I miss you, Saint," Josephine purred in French.

"Wish I could say the same."

"Ouch. I forgot how wicked your tongue can be."

"I really can't talk right now."

"Don't want to keep Miss Olivia Martin waiting?"

"Josephine—"

"Shhh, my love. Just remember who you belong to. And remember our agreement."

"My name is Clayton Andrews. I'm a math teacher, and that's it."

"And if I hear any different…"

"Goodbye, Josephine."

"Goodbye, my beautiful Saint."

Saint folded the phone up and threw it over the balcony.

Petrescu had to be held up by two blondes as they made their way to his suite.

"You had too much to drink, Laurent," one of the women said.

"Nonsense," he replied with a wave of his hand. "I always walk this way."

They all laughed.

"Would one of you lovely ladies be so kind as to reach into my pocket and retrieve the key to my suite?"

The blonde on his right dug into his pocket and pulled out the key. She swiped it through the slot.

"Let me warn you," Petrescu said to the blondes as they stumbled through the door. "Coursing through these veins is pure Rumanian blood and pure Viagra."

Instead of chuckling at his wisecrack, the blondes stared at the sofa. Petrescu followed their gaze and sobered up quickly.

"Saint, my friend. You come for the after party?"

"Ladies, this is a private party. So, if you don't mind letting yourselves out."

Petrescu started to back out of the suite.

"Don't make me shoot you," Saint told him, tapping the object concealed under a newspaper resting on his lap.

"No, Saint, of course not. I was just seeing the lovely ladies out. Go!" He ushered them out and closed the door.

"Saint–"

Saint was on his feet and charging at Petrescu before he had a chance to shit himself. He grabbed him by the front of his tux and slammed him against the wall.

"You take-it-in-the-ass, cum-drinking, snitch, rat bastard."

"How dare you call me a snitch, rat bastard."

"Who else would tell Josephine that I was here?"

"Saint, please. You know as well as I do that if I didn't tell her and she found out by someone else, she would've hung me off the Eiffel Tower by my nut sac."

"What did you tell her?"

"I just told her that you were here with Glenn and some friends having a good time."

"What else?" Saint asked, pressing him harder against the wall.

"That's all, I swear."

"How did she know Miss Martin's name?"

"You know Josephine. She wanted to run a check on her to make sure she was squeaky clean. To make sure you weren't... back in the business."

"The business? Is that what you call what I used to do?"

Petrescu shrugged. "It was just business, right?"

Saint backed away from him. Petrescu looked down at the newspaper and realized that the object Saint had been concealing was not a gun, but the suite's telephone receiver.

"What's the real deal with Marion Claude?"

"Do you really want to know?"

Saint rubbed his temples. "Is it safe for him to come to Miss Martin's salon?"

"No one will dare make an attempt on his life in America."

"And you're sure about that?"

"I'll bet my life on it."

"Don't give me any ideas," Saint said, and with that, he exited the suite.

Three hours later, Glenn returned. Saint was stretched out on the couch with a wet cloth over his face. He looked up when he heard the suite's door open. He put the cloth back over his head when he saw Glenn.

"Please tell me that wasn't who I think it was on the phone earlier," Glenn said, plopping down on the couch next to Saint's feet.

"My head is pounding right now."

"Petrescu snitched you out, didn't he?"

"You know he did, thinking he would score some points with Josephine."

"Did you convince her that you're only here because of me?"

"That's what I told her, but is she convinced? I don't know."

"Saint, I'm real sorry for putting you in this predicament."

"It's not your fault. You had no way of knowing that Petrescu was going to be here. This was supposed to be a get-together for fashion designers, not for Rumanian mob accountants masquerading as tailors."

"What do you think Josephine's going to do?"

"For now, nothing. She's like a Venus flytrap. She won't snap her lobes shut until she's sure she's got you."

"What are you going to do?"

"I'm not doing anything wrong. So, I'm going to keep doing what I'm doing. If I change up, she'll definitely think something's up."

The suite's phone rang twice before Glenn answered it.

"Hello...yes, he's right here." He held the phone out toward Saint. "It's Olivia."

Saint took the wet cloth off his face and grabbed the phone from him. "What's up, barber girl?"

"Just calling to say goodnight."

"That's so sweet." Saint shooed at Glenn like he was an annoying fly so he could have some privacy.

"And I wanted to say thank you for getting Marion Claude, his entire entourage, and the other designers to fly all the way to New York City just to visit my little ol' salon. And you did it without handing out a single business card."

"You don't have to thank me. I really want to see you prosper. It's not every day that I meet a woman of your caliber."

"You got me blushing right now." Olivia couldn't remember the last time she expressed her feelings to a man without being guarded. "So, tell me, Clayton, what should I be expecting on Monday? There has to be at least twenty-five people coming, right?"

"Expect forty. And that's not counting the reporters."

"Where am I supposed to put all those people?"

"You have a waiting area, don't you?"

"I have two. Each can hold about fifteen people."

"Fifteen in each, that's thirty. Then you'll have some in chairs getting haircuts, manicures, pedicures, etc. Don't worry about accommodating the reporters. They'll be happy just to get interviews and photographs."

"Anything else I should prepare for?"

"Yes. Keep in mind that you're not charging them anything, but the gifts they are going to shower you with will more than make up for it. Expect everything from jewelry to clothes. And while the reporters are there, expect Marion Claude and everyone else to treat you like y'all are the best of friends."

"Anything else?"

"One last thing. When this fiasco is over and everything calms down, I want a haircut."

Olivia smiled. "Sure, I'll tell Grace—"

"Don't play yourself. I want you to cut my hair, Miss You'll-never-find-a-barber-like-me."

"I thought you liked walking around with half-done tapers and uneven hair."

"You're a barber *and* a comedian? Where have you been all my life?"

Olivia closed her eyes and smiled because she was just thinking the same thing. "Clayton, I'm going to let you go."

"Thanks for tucking me in."

"Grace and I are going shopping in the afternoon, so I'll see you at the club tomorrow night."

"The club? Tomorrow night?"

"That's what Glenn said."

"Riight, the club tomorrow night," Saint said, making a mental note to snuff Glenn as soon as he saw him again.

"Goodnight, Clayton."

"Goodnight, Olivia."

"So exactly when were you going to tell me about the club?" Saint asked Glenn the following afternoon over lunch.

"I wasn't. I knew if I had asked you, you would've told me you don't do clubs. Never have; never will. But, if Olivia mentioned it—"

"You conniving lil'...I think I'm starting to rub off on you."

"C'mon, Saint. It's just a club."

Saint stared at him.

"I'm going to make my move tonight with Grace."

"In the club?"

"No, the club is just to...you know."

"No, I don't."

"Damn, Saint, to be so smart you are so out of touch. The club is where it all starts. You and your date have a few drinks, then hit the dance floor. You dance, talk, touch, and test the waters."

"Test the waters?"

"You know. You're dancing, doing your thing, and then you turn her around and grind up on her. If she backs that thang up, it's on. If she lets you run your hands all over her, it's on. But the deal sealer is when her hand grazes your crotch. Then it's time to go, because it's ON *AND* POPPING."

"It sounds like you're having sex with clothes on."

"I never looked at it like that before."

"So when I see Grace grab your crotch—"

"No, you freak. I didn't tell you all that so you could be staring at my crotch all night."

"Why did you tell me *all that* then?"

"So you could be on point with Olivia."

Saint's mouth dropped open. "Olivia doesn't strike me to be the type to be backing anything up, and even if she was, she wouldn't be backing it up on me. I don't dance."

"C'mon, Saint, you're always complaining about how boring your new life is. Now you have the chance to do something different."

"That's what I'm afraid of."

The club scene was a paranoid man's worst nightmare. The strobe lights, pounding music, people jerking and popping their bodies to the music. Too many dark spots for people who didn't want to be seen. Dark spots Saint had occupied too many times in his previous life. He thought about backing out at the last minute, but when Grace and Olivia showed up at the suite, Olivia took his breath away. She was wearing a sleeveless, pleated dress by Tommy Hilfiger; the simplicity of it is what made her look so beautiful. It was the first time he saw the carefree Olivia and not Olivia, the businesswoman.

Grace wore a white and lavender tennis skirt with a white Polo shirt. Saint could hear Glenn's heart pounding. Saint was dressed casual in a pair of Akademik jeans, a white Phat Farm fitted T-shirt, and a pair of Rockport's.

As they walked deeper into Light Nightclub, which was located inside the Bellagio Hotel, Saint's eyes darted from side to side behind his lightly-tinted Paul Smith's. DJ Kris Cut was the man behind the sounds and the one responsible for the ballers and beautiful women shaking it up on the dance floor.

The four of them found room at the bar and ordered drinks.

"It's got to be at least eighty-five degrees in here," Olivia said, taking a sip of her drink.

"Perfect for dancing," Grace said, downing her drink. "Hurry up and drink so we can hit the dance floor, Glenn."

After finishing his drink in three gulps, Glenn let Grace lead him to the dance floor.

"I'm going to tell you now," Saint said, finishing his drink and signaling the bartender for another. "It's going to take more than one drink to get me out there."

"I haven't danced in…" Olivia paused for a moment, trying to remember. "I don't know how long. Not in public anyway." Sensing Saint's discomfort, she asked, "Are you okay?"

"I don't get out much."

"C'mon." Olivia grabbed him by the hand.

"I don't dance."

"What? C'mon, everybody knows how to dance."

"I didn't say I don't know how to dance. I said I *don't* dance."

Olivia took off his glasses, folded them, and hung them on the front of her dress. "Will you please dance with me?"

Saint looked into her puppy dog eyes. He then looked in the direction of the dance floor and saw Glenn making a fool of himself. His face softened; Olivia smiled. Taking his hand once again, she led him to the dance floor.

"Steam" by Nicole Scherzinger from The Pussycat Dolls pumped through the speakers. Olivia started swaying her hips to the beat as they made their way to the dance floor. Saint was mesmerized. Olivia looked over her shoulder and caught him staring at her butt. She smiled; Saint's face turned red.

Grace threw her hands in the air and waved to Olivia and Saint. Olivia waved back. She turned to face Saint and locked eyes with him as she allowed her body to feel the music. Saint broke out in a two-step.

Thirty steps later, Olivia pulled Saint's ear to her lips. "Is that all you know how to do?"

"Oh, you want me to come out the stash on you? Okay."

Saint continued the two-step and then added a dip to it. Olivia started laughing. Saint held his finger up for her to watch his next dance move. His two-step transitioned into a two-step with a shake, then a two-step with a stutter step. They both busted out laughing.

"You so stupid, Clayton."

"Don't be hating on my two-step," Saint said, then looked over at Glenn and shook his head. Glenn looked like he was doing a combination of the running man and the cabbage patch.

"Checking Me" by Bobby Valentino blended into the mix. Saint felt Olivia dance closer to him. He tried matching his rhythm with hers. She nodded. He winked. She turned her back to him. He stopped breathing. She bent over at the waist and touched her toes, then slowly stood up while rotating her hips. Saint stopped holding his breath when she turned around.

"Only Want To Be Your Lover" by Mary J. Blige played next. Saint kept in step with Olivia as she bounced, dipped, and swayed. He read her lips as she sang along with the chorus.

"Boy, I want to be your lover, only want to be your friend. Let me be the one who loves ya; want to be your best friend."

She turned her back to him and…backed that thang up, parking it on him. Saint's hands found themselves on her hips. Olivia placed her hands on top of his. Saint's lips brushed the side of her neck. With a moan, she wrapped herself with his arms.

Saint felt himself rising as he crushed Olivia's body into his and inhaled her scent. Olivia felt the rise, as well, but instead of pulling away from it, she grinded into it more. And then it happened. As she turned to face him, her hand glided across his manhood. It happened so quick that he thought he had imagined it. The second time she did it, it was slow and with an exclamation mark. From there, it was *ON AND POPPING*. Olivia's lips met Saint's as he leaned in to kiss her. For the next three songs, they didn't say a word. All they did was dance and kiss.

"We're out of here," Glenn said, walking past Olivia and Saint.

Grace whispered something in Olivia's ear before catching up with Glenn.

"What was that about?" Saint asked.

"She told me not to come back to the suite tonight."

"Oh well, I guess you're just stuck with me and my two-step."

"Let's get out of here."

"I got the perfect place," Saint said with a wink.

Olivia kicked off her shoes and sat on the plush couch in Saint's suite while he fixed them a drink. He returned a few minutes later. Olivia looked up at him as he stood in front of her, not moving.

"What?"

"You are so beautiful."

Olivia got up from the sofa, stood on her toes, and kissed him. Saint broke away from her long enough to put the drinks on the table. Then he swept her off her feet. Their lips locked as he carried her off to the bedroom, where he laid her down on the king-sized bed and slowly lowered himself on top of her. Olivia moaned as she met his thrusts. In the dimly lit room, Saint sat up on his knees between her legs and stared down at her. She was breathing hard, looking at him with hunger in her eyes. He reached under her dress and ran his hands up the backs of her thighs. Her flesh was so soft that it gave him goose bumps. He interlaced his fingers in the waistline of her panties and slowly began pulling them down. Olivia made it easy for him by lifting her butt in the air. He blinked when her hands clamped down on his.

"Do you have anything?" she asked.

Saint closed his eyes for a moment and then opened them. "No. I didn't expect…I didn't plan on being with you."

Olivia smiled. "I want to kill you for getting me all worked up and not being able to finish the job. On the other hand, if you would've gone into the drawer of that nightstand and pulled out a condom, I would've thought you planned this all along. Then, I would've wanted to kill you."

"So, no matter how you look at it, you want to kill me right now."

"In the worst way."

"I got an idea." Saint sat with his back against the headboard. "Sit in between my legs."

Olivia looked at him suspiciously.

"Trust me."

She got up and moved in between his legs. He then pulled her back against his chest.

"What most people don't know," he said, while pressing his fingertips into the muscles of her upper back and shoulders, "is that most of the body's tension is stored right here in the trapeziuses."

She winched as his fingertips penetrated deeper. She was about to tell him to ease up, but then it felt like someone had pulled the plug and years of tenseness started draining from her body, leaving her relaxed and weak.

"God, this feels better than sex," she expressed, her eyes rolling to the back of her head. The last thing Olivia remembered before drifting off into a deep sleep was Saint nibbling on her ear.

While staring down at her, Saint gently moved the strands of hair covering the sides of her face. He closed his eyes, and like a blind man, he let his remaining four senses become his sight. He traced the contours of her face with the back of his hand, etching every crease and crevice into his memory. He listened to her slow, rhythmic breathing as her chest slightly rose and fell. Then he inhaled her, separating her true scent from the traces of perfume still lingering on her. Her scent reminded him of the first droplets before a heavy rain. Then with a feather's touch, he ran the tip of his tongue down the side of her neck. Olivia stirred and then opened her eyes.

"Oh my God. I can't believe I fell asleep on you like that," she said in a groggy voice.

Saint made her turn over as he laid flat on his back. He patted his chest. She smiled and snuggled up against him, placing her head on his chest.

"Clayton." Her voice was just above a whisper.

"Yes."

"Say something in French."

She smiled as he rattled off a sentence.

"I don't know what you said, but it sounded sexy as hell."

"Love has reasons that Reason can't understand," he translated.

"Umm, that's deep."

"You're deep."

Olivia drifted back to sleep, leaving Saint in the middle of a battle between his head and his heart. His head warned him that this was all wrong. That the longer Olivia stayed in his presence, the greater danger she'd be in. His heart wanted to forget everything and just focus on the present, then take it from there. He knew from past experience that emotions couldn't be trusted. He had to go with his head, but tonight, he would enjoy the moment. Tomorrow, they would be on Mr. Seeger's jet back to New York. Monday, he would make sure everything ran smoothly; and Tuesday, he would be out of her life forever.

Chapter 5

"You're really starting to freak me out," Grace said as Olivia pulled out of J.F.K. Airport.

"What are you talking about?"

"I'm talking about you being quieter than usual."

"I just got a lot on my mind," Olivia told her. "I'm thinking of what I have to do to prepare for tomorrow."

"You do know who you're talking to, right? You know you can't feed me that line of crap. What happened between you and Clayton last night?"

A smile the size of the sun appeared on Olivia's face.

"The sex was like that?"

"What we did was better than sex."

"Girl, there ain't nothing better than sex."

"Before last night, I would've agreed with you."

"What...in...the...world? What did he do to you?" Grace pressed, wanting the details.

Olivia's thoughts took her back to last night. The way Saint had swept her off her feet and whisked her to the bedroom. The way he had been so gentle with her. The way he had her on fire, and then just as she was about to throw caution to the wind and let him sex her without a condom, he switched gears on her. The magic in his hands with just a simple shoulder massage. *Oh God, did he know?* She tried not to let on. She tried to lay as still as possible as her legs spasmed and she...

"Olivia!" Grace said.

Olivia had run a red light, causing an oncoming car to skid to a halt. The irate driver laid on his horn.

Olivia swerved. "Fucking asshole!"

Grace's eyes were as big as saucers. Not only at the fact that they had almost been in an accident, but because Olivia had cursed. She watched Olivia turn the air conditioner on full-blast and then let down all the windows.

"Giiirl, we is going to my grandmama's house Monday afternoon when all this is over," Grace told her.

"For what?"

"That man done put some roots on you."

"I'm going to ask Grace to marry me," Glenn said as Saint pulled up to Glenn's apartment building.

"You can't be serious."

"I love her, Saint."

"Did you love her before or after she rocked your world?"

"I was in love with her before she rocked my world, but after... I need her in my life forever."

"I think you're thinking with the little head."

"Nah, Saint. We made a connection last night."

"Yeah, your dick in her pussy."

"I'm dead serious right now."

Saint stared at him for a moment. "And when are you supposed to be asking her to marry you?"

"As soon as I buy the ring."

"And when is that?"

"This might not be the right time, but I need a loan."

"Oh, hell no!"

"C'mon, I'm your boy. You know I'm good for it. I'm about to be the next icon of fashion."

"I don't care if you were going to be the next president of the United States."

"Saint—"

"No."

"But—"

"No."

"Saint!"

"No! I'm not giving you money for a ring. If you two made a connection like you claim, she would marry you without a ring."

"I can't believe you're going to deny me."

"And I can't believe you're going to give your heart to a woman you barely know."

"A woman I barely know? That's why you won't help me out? You think… Grace isn't *HER*. She's not going to stab me in the chest with a six-inch dagger."

"This has nothing to do with *HER*, so don't even go there. I just don't want any parts of it."

"Any parts of it?"

"It's going to start off with me giving you the money for the ring, and then, you're going to ask me to be your best man."

"You wouldn't be my best man?"

"Then you're going to have your kids calling me Uncle Clayton."

"That's what normal people do, Saint."

"I'm not normal! My life was never normal, and it will never be normal. Do you really want your family around me? Think about that real hard. Grace and your children would only be more pawns that Josephine would use to control me. Do you want your future family to be treated as pawns?"

Glenn looked out the car window, and without looking back at Saint, he responded, "You're my best friend. And I love Grace. So, what you're indirectly telling me is if I marry her, our friendship will end only because you wouldn't want us entangled in your screwed up life?"

"Follow you heart, Glenn. Friends come and go, but true love..."

Glenn took a deep breath and opened the car door. "You're right. If she really loves me, she won't worry about some stupid ring, right?"

"Think of it as the first test of the many you will give her."

"No, Saint. Normal people don't test the ones they love."

Saint pulled up his shirt and ran his fingers across the keloid on his chest.

"Like I said, Saint, *normal* people."

Early Monday morning, news reporters who looked like they had camped out in front of the salon all night greeted Olivia. She smiled and answered a couple of questions before unlocking the shutters and walking in. Grace, Miki, and Baby walked in ten minutes later. The rest of Olivia's staff, which included Chuck, Esther, and Jordan, arrived a half hour later.

Olivia's heart was beating a million miles a minute. She kept going over every single detail to make sure she didn't miss anything. When she called Saint's cell phone, she got no answer.

"Grace, call Glenn and see if they are on their way."

"You must've talked them up," Grace said, looking toward the front door.

Glenn walked in cheesing for the cameras and wearing a corduroy outfit with a checkerboard design. On the back of the jacket, the words "KING ME" were written in gold lettering.

When Olivia didn't see Saint, she bit on her bottom lip and pulled Glenn away from one of the reporters.

"Where's Clayton?" she inquired.

"He'll be here. He had to...stop by the office first."

"Stop by the office?"

"Yeah. He had some last-minute paperwork he needed to get to his people."

"Miss Clark," Saint said, handing the seventeen-year-old, mother of two her test paper, "I'm proud of you."

"An eighty-five, Mr. Andrews? Oh my God! I can't believe it. This is the highest grade I ever got on a test. Thank you, Mr. Andrews."

"Don't thank me. I didn't pass the test. You did."

"But it was your teaching—"

Saint cut her off. "It was your dedication. You proved to yourself that you got it in you." He looked down at the next test in his hand. "Mrs. Ramos," he said, giving the middle-aged Spanish woman a suspicious look.

"Mr. Andrews, you know my English isn't very good and—"

Saint held his hand up. "I know you're not giving me an excuse, Mrs. Ramos. In this class, what did we say an excuse is?"

"It's a pretty word for bullshit."

"Hmmm. So, what were you saying?"

"Nothing, Mr. Andrews."

Saint handed her the test paper.

"My God," she said, putting her hand to her chest. Then she looked for the name at the top of paper to make sure it was hers. "Eighty-four, Mr. Andrews?"

"Congratulations."

Mrs. Ramos stood up and hugged him. She said a prayer for him in Spanish and then kissed his hands.

"You did it. Mrs. Ramos. All I did was convince you that you could do it."

Saint saw Mr. Reed stiffen, knowing he was the only one who hadn't received his test yet.

"Mr. Reed," Saint said, walking toward him, "I see our little talk went a long way." Saint handed over his test.

"Get the fuck out of here!" Mr. Reed jumped out of his chair. "You fucking with me, right?"

"No, I'm not messing with you."

"This has to be a mistake."

"That's what Principal Baker said, until he checked the test himself."

The nineteen-year-old held up his paper for the others to see the big 100 at the top of his paper in red ink and with a personal congratulation from Mr. Baker. Everyone in the class stood up and clapped.

Saint curled and uncurled his toes in his shoes, willing the tears that were forming at the corners of his eyes not to fall.

He batted them away as Mr. Reed shook his hand and gave him a bear hug.

"All right, let's settle down for a moment," Saint said, looking at his watch. "I have to leave early today. This test you took is way harder than the GED. The test you took was taken from first-year college textbooks."

"You're serious?" Miss Clark asked.

"Trust me; I made the test up myself. So y'all know what that means, right?"

"That means I'm going to pass that GED with flying colors," Mr. Reed replied.

"No, that means each one of you are going to pass that GED with flying colors. I'm putting all of you in for the test. It's going to be in two weeks," Saint told them as he looked at his watch again.

"You must have a hot date, Mr. Andrews," Mr. Reed said.

"Yeah, I got a date with my barber."

Saint pulled up to his apartment. He unbuttoned his white shirt and started unbuckling his khakis with one hand while inserting his key into the front door with the other. He had ten minutes to transform from math teacher to corporate accountant. His suit, tie, shoes, and briefcase were already laid out on the bed. His house phone rang, interrupting his progress.

"Glenn, I'm on my way."

"I'm about to have a nervous breakdown. I've been trying to reach you all morning."

Saint was taken off guard hearing Olivia's voice. Only two people had his home number.

"I'll be there before they show up. Don't worry. Put Glenn on the phone." Saint could hear her handing the phone to him.

"Clayton—"

"Glenn, I'm going to kill you."

"Whoa! I didn't give her your home number. I dialed it on my cell and then handed it to her."

"I can't talk now. I have to finish getting dressed. I'll be there in a few."

"What if Claude and the rest of them get here before you?"

Saint looked at the cheap Timex on his wrist. "It's only a quarter to twelve. Claude is going to want to show up in the middle of the afternoon, between one and two, when the streets are the most crowded."

"Has to make a grand entrance, huh?"

"Don't hate on him. You'll be doing the same thing soon."

"Fuck you, Saint."

"I love you, too."

Saint hung up, took off the Timex, and threw it on the pile of math teacher clothes. He grabbed his Omega Speedmaster off the dresser along with his Giorgio Armani prescription glasses. Then he took a look at himself in the mirror.

"You're enjoying this, aren't you?"

"This is the most excitement we've had in a long time."

"Well, don't get used to it. After today, it's over."

"Really?"

"Really."

"Glenn is talking marriage, and you're going to end it with Olivia before y'all even get a chance to get started? Damn, Saint, you're going to go back to being alone."

"I won't be alone. I have you to talk to."

"Talking to yourself doesn't count."

"Then I'll get a plant."

"People will think you're crazy if they see you talking to a plant."

"Can't be any crazier than talking to myself in the mirror."

"You got a point there."

Saint arrived in downtown Manhattan at twelve-thirty. As soon as he turned off Madison, he saw it and was impressed. Butta Cutz didn't match the picture he had of it in his head. Before driving down the block to park, he noticed a couple reporters milling around the salon, waiting for the man of the hour to arrive. He exited his car, grabbing his briefcase from the passenger's side, and headed up the block. As he got a couple feet away from the salon, his cell phone vibrated.

"Hello."

"Where are you?" Olivia asked.

"I'm walking through the door right now."

Olivia whipped her head around. If Saint didn't have the phone to his ear, she wouldn't have recognized him. It was amazing how something as insignificant as a pair of glasses and a briefcase could change the appearance of a person. Miki was on him like a cheap suit.

"You are definitely not a news reporter," she said, twirling a strand of her hair between her fingers.

"No, I'm not."

"No, he's not," Olivia said, walking up and interrupting the conversation. "Mr. Andrews, I need to see you in my office."

"Yes, Miss Martin." Saint adjusted his glasses and followed Olivia to the back.

The way she addressed him had turned him on. He was now seeing another side of her. The strictly professional side; the side running a million-dollar business. Dressed in a pair of black slacks, a black turtleneck, and a pair of open-toed shoes, she certainly looked the part.

She entered her office and held the door for him. Saint walked in. A quick glance around told him that Olivia definitely had an eye for decorating. She closed the door. Before Saint had a chance to set his briefcase down, Olivia walked over and wrapped her arms around his waist.

"Miss Martin—"

"Oh shut up, Clayton, and just hold me."

"Everything's going to be fine, Olivia."

She looked up at him. "I didn't know you wore prescription glasses. You look good in them, in a Clarke Kent kind of way."

"Are you calling me your Superman?"

Olivia pushed him away from her and walked around her desk to have a seat. Saint put his briefcase down, followed her around her desk, and stood behind her chair. He gently placed his hands on her shoulders. Olivia had a flashback and started to stand up, but Saint held her down.

"Girl, you're so tense. I won't put you to sleep this time. I promise."

Olivia stopped moving and let Saint do his thing. She felt the stress quickly leaving her shoulders. His fingertips didn't tickle her soul the way they had done the other night, but they still brought a smile to her face.

Her intercom chirped.

"Olivia, Jon-Jon is here," Miki announced.

"Tell him I'm too busy to mess with him today."

"He's jumping down my throat about you interviewing a Lynise Rogers for a job."

"Oh, God," Olivia sighed.

"I'll be outside waiting on Marion Claude," Saint told her. "We will continue this at a later time."

Saint didn't respond. He just picked up his briefcase and walked out.

"Miki, send my brother in."

A few minutes later, Jon-Jon walked in with his college girlfriend. Olivia was impressed. She appeared to be twenty-four or twenty-five, slim, and sophisticated looking. She was rocking a pair of army fatigue boy shorts, showcasing her long legs, and a matching vest. But what caught Olivia's attention were her shoes. Olivia was a shoe connoisseur. Lynise had on a pair of El Dantés.

"Sis, this is Lynise."

Olivia stood up to shake her hand.

"Nice to meet you, Miss Martin," Lynise said with an accent Olivia couldn't quite place.

"What you got going on today, sis? You got reporters and everything out there. You got Puffy coming down? Oh shit! That's what I'm talking about. Yeah!"

"Calm down, Jon-Jon. Puffy isn't coming here. I got some people from overseas coming."

"They got it going on like Puffy?"

"Listen, I'm kind of busy right now—"

"C'mon, sis. Lynise took off from school to come down here. Don't hit me with the 'come back tomorrow' line. You don't even have to interview her. You're just going through the motions anyway, right? She can start right now. It looks like you're going to need all the help you can get today."

Olivia leaned back in her chair. "Did you bring your résumé?"

"Ah—"

"Here's her résumé," Jon-Jon said, pointing to his braids. Lynise had braided his hair in the fashion of a spider web.

"A lot of the work I did was under the table," she said.

"Well, everything here is done above the table."

"Yes, I know. I'm dying to get a real paycheck."

"Okay, so you braid hair. What else?"

"I do manicures, pedicures, weaves, fusions—"

"We don't do weaves and fusions here." Olivia pressed the button on her intercom. "Miki, send Baby in here."

Baby knocked on the door a minute later and stuck her head in. "What's up, boss?"

"This is Lynise. We're going to be extremely busy today and she needs a job. So, I'm going to give her a try."

"On a day like today?" Baby asked, sounding as if she might be in disagreement with Olivia's decision but knowing she didn't have much say.

"Yes, today."

"Whatever you say, ma."

"Thank you, Miss Martin," Lynise said.

"Call me Olivia."

"C'mon," Baby said to Lynise. "I'll show you around, introduce you to the rest of the team, and then show you my station."

Jon-Jon hugged Olivia. "I love you, sis."

"I need you to be on your best behavior today."

"C'mon, this is me you talking to," Jon-Jon said, beating his chest.

"David, Mike, and Shawn said they're going to stop by later."

"They the ones you need to be telling to be on their best behavior, especially Mike. He thinks he's the shit now because he got a license to walk around with a gun."

"Work with me, Jon-Jon."

"I got you, sis. Don't even worry about it."

"Now, if you don't mind, I have to finish meeting with Clayton."

"The dude that left the office when we came in?"

"Yes."

"He's the accountant?"

"Not today, Jon-Jon."

"Sis, I'm on my best behavior." He opened the door and looked both ways. He spotted Saint talking with Glenn, and when he made eye contact with him, he called him over. As Saint walked into the office, Jon-Jon closed the door.

"What's up, duke?"

"Hi."

"You seeing my sister?"

"Jon-Jon–" Olivia started.

Jon-Jon held his hand up for her not to interrupt him.

"I think you need to ask your sister that."

"I'm asking you, duke."

Saint didn't respond.

Jon-Jon looked him up and down. "You got a business card or something?"

"I don't use business cards."

"So how can people get in touch with you?"

"My clients know how to get in touch with me."

"What about a person who's not one of your clients?"

"Then we don't have anything to talk about."

"You sure you ain't a lawyer, 'cause you got a slick mouth?"

"Jon-Jon!" Olivia started walking toward him.

"All right, all right. I'm out of here," he said, opening the door and letting himself out.

Saint folded his arms. "I like him already."

At one o'clock on the dot, a fleet of Mercedes limos turned off of Madison. Saint knew they were there by the way the reporters started scrambling. Quadruplet blonde bombshells stepped out of the first limo wearing dresses designed by Laurent Petrescu. The women stood on each side of the door as Petrescu stepped out holding the hand of a bombshell that looked like the first four. The women were in fact quintuplets. Cameras were clicking, and reporters talked into their mini tape recorders. Out of the next three limos emerged mixed couples of different nationalities. The last ones to exit the limos were the designers of the fashions that the models were showcasing. The last, and the longest, limo dramatically rolled up. The chauffeur stepped out and walked around to the backdoor, but didn't open it until he heard a soft tap on the window.

As he swung the door open, a set of extremely long legs appeared. The face of the woman to whom they belong to finally came into view. The Glamazon was six-two with blue eyes and flaming red hair. Everyone's attention focused again on the door as another set of long legs stepped out onto the sidewalk. An exact replica of the Glamazon exited the limo and stood to her full six-two height. Both women wore identical body-hugging dresses. Long slits up the sides let everyone know the Glamazon twins were wearing French-cut panties. Both women stood on the sidewalk awaiting the appearance of their benefactor.

Marion Claude stepped out of the limo greeting the cameras with the Miss America wave. Reporters shot a couple questions at him, to which he only smiled in response and pretended to be looking for someone.

"I do not know how you found out that I would be here," he said with a surprised look. "I am here only to visit a *very* dear friend of mine, Miss Olivia Martin. Now, if you will excuse me."

Marion Claude looped his arms around the waists of the flaming redhead, supermodel twins and headed for Butta Cutz. Olivia greeted him at the door. He embraced her and kissed her on both cheeks like they'd known each other for years.

Before he pulled away from her, he whispered in her ear, "I'm impressed. I was expecting only a couple reporters."

Olivia winked at him as she ushered him inside.

She introduced all of her employees to Marion Claude, and Marion Claude introduced them to the other fashion designers. Marion Claude complimented Olivia on the decorations and even commented loud enough for the reporters to hear.

"Anyone who does not come to Butta Cutz is not worth the air he breathes. This is the Mecca of men salons in the West."

He looked to the front door and waved for the men with boxes in their hands to come in. Men, who looked to be second-string models, brought in boxes of various sizes. Now it was Olivia's turn to act surprised. Marion Claude insisted she open them right there in the reception area. When she opened the first one, she didn't have to act surprised anymore. The first box contained a dress with a design so intricate that she knew it was one of a kind. The next was a velvet box from Petrescu. Olivia opened it and found herself at a loss for words. Baby, Grace, and Esther were stunned. Olivia pulled out the tennis bracelet and marveled at the different color stones glistening in the sunlight. Olivia knew how much something like that cost. What she didn't know was how could Petrescu afford to just give it to her as a gift? With every box she opened, the cameras were steadily clicking away, and Marion Claude was right by her side.

After Marion Claude's "gift extravaganza", he removed his jacket and allowed Olivia to lead him to her chair. She was instructing Grace and the rest of her team to tend to the others, when Marion Claude stopped her.

"Don't worry about them," he told her. "They're only here as decorations."

Olivia looked around and noticed that's exactly what they looked like. Everyone had picked a spot in the salon to stand or sit, and they performed for the cameras and crowd.

Marion allowed one reporter to interview him as Olivia cut his hair. He spoke of his humble beginnings as a salesman in a shabby fabric store in Paris. He then went to Baby's station where she prepped him for a manicure and pedicure. Baby tended to his hands while Lynise worked on his feet. Olivia stood by and watched to see if Lynise knew what she was doing. Liking what she saw, Olivia nodded her head in approval.

Saint sat at the reception desk with Miki naming the hottest clubs in Japan. While going back and forth with her, he kept his eyes roving on everything and everyone. All the while, Jon-Jon kept his eyes on him. Saint knew he was clocking him, but he didn't let on.

Saint caught movement at the front door. When a burly cop walked in, he had to calm his nerves and remind himself that he wasn't carrying.

Jon-Jon saw the police officer at the same time Saint did. A big smile grew on his face. He gorilla-walked to the cop, giving him a pound and a hug once he reached him. He whispered something to the cop while pointing over his shoulder in Saint's direction. The cop locked eyes with Saint and nodded slowly. The beast in the cop uniform softened when Olivia ran over and hugged him.

That must be brother number two, Saint thought.

Olivia looked his way and winked. He adjusted his glasses and gave her a little wave. One of the flaming redheads walked over to Olivia and whispered something to her, and Olivia followed her to Baby's workstation. Marion Claude said something to Olivia, which made her look in Saint's direction. She nodded and then walked toward him.

Saint bristled.

"Marion Claude said he would like to talk to you in private. I told him that the two of you could use my office."

"Did he say what he wanted to talk about?"

"No. You can wait in my office. Baby's just about finished with him. I'll send him in."

"Okay."

Ten minutes later, Marion Claude walked in.

"Mr. Andrews," he said, extending his hand.

Saint shook it.

"I am honored to be breathing the same air as you." Marion sat on the sofa and looked him up and down. "When I got a call from Josephine telling me that the man sitting at my table selling me a dress was her infamous Saint, I nearly shitted my pants."

Saint refrained from showing any emotion to the apparent sign of respect.

"But, she assured me that you weren't there on business."

"What else did she tell you?"

"She told me to behave myself."

"Are you?"

"I have to now that I know the eyes of the Saint are on me."

What? Saint screamed in his head. *Josephine, what the fuck did you tell this man?*

"You no doubt know that I am a very wealthy man. Anything in the world I want, I can have. ANYTHING," Marion Claude stressed.

"I don't see how that's any of my business, but I'm sure you're about to connect the dots for me."

"Name your price from one to infinity, and I swear on my mother's grave…may God rest her soul…I won't argue with you. It will be in your account with just one phone call from me."

"I don't need money."

"What about power?"

"I almost made you shit your pants. I think I have enough power."

Marion smiled. "You're that loyal to Josephine?"

"No, I just don't like you."

Marion busted out laughing. "I can have you and everyone in this salon killed with a snap of a finger."

"And I can kill you with the pull of a finger," Saint said, aiming an imaginary gun at him and pulling the trigger.

"And how will you make it out of here alive?"

"I'll walk out the front door."

"Impossible!"

"Doing the impossible is what makes me the best at what I do."

Marion regarded him curiously and then busted out laughing again. "I'm just messing with you."

"I think it's time for you and your people to go. You've kept your end of the deal by stopping by."

"Yes, I have. And I do have a couple more stops to make before I prepare to fly back to France."

"Have a safe flight home," Saint said, extending his hand.

Marion grabbed it and stood up. "If you ever change your mind—"

"Goodbye, Mr. Claude."

After Marion Claude left, Olivia came in with the boxes of gifts and placed them on her desk. "Can you believe all of this?"

"I told you what to expect."

"Yes, but there are pieces of jewelry here that costs over a thousand dollars."

"It didn't cost them a penny. They get that stuff for free. Jewelers give them pieces for their models to wear. For every piece a jeweler gives them, they're guaranteed at least twenty sales."

"After today, my salon is going to be the hottest spot in the country. Thank you, Clayton."

"You don't have to thank me."

"No, I do."

She walked up to him and ran both of her hands up his chest and around his shoulders. Then she stood on her tiptoes and kissed him. Saint stood ridged, but the softness of her lips... He leaned into her and held her tight as he kissed her back.

"Yo, sis," Jon-Jon said, opening the door and starting to walk in.

"Jon-Jon! What I tell you about barging into my office?"

Saint pulled away from her.

"Damn, sis, this is your office, not your bedroom."

"I think I better go," Saint said, heading out.

Jon-Jon gave him a hard stare. "I got my eye on you, bean counter," he warned, then bumped Saint as he walked by.

Saint exited the salon in time to see Marion Claude climbing into his limo. Marion waved at him. Saint restrained himself from sticking up his middle finger.

"What's up, chief?"

Saint looked around and saw brother number two.

"My name's Mike, but people around here call me Big Mike," he said, extending his ham-sized hand toward Saint.

"Clayton Andrews," Saint replied as he watched his hand disappear into the palm of the giant's hand.

Big Mike squeezed his hand a little harder than normal, while making one of his pecs jump. Saint bit his tongue to keep from laughing in his face.

"I'd hate to be on the wrong side of one of them clubs," Saint commented with a smile.

"It wouldn't be a pretty sight, especially for somebody with a pretty face like yourself."

"I'm a law-abiding citizen, so I won't have to worry about that."

"You try to play my sister and a busted face will be the least of your injuries."

Saint seized the opening and took it. "First, your brother in there threatens me, and now you threaten me. I don't take too kindly to threats."

Mike folded his arms across his chest. "I don't care what you don't take too kindly to."

"You know what? I don't have to take this. Tell your sister it was nice knowing her."

"It will be my pleasure, pretty boy."

Saint stormed off. That was the easy part. The hard part would be having the willpower not to answer his cell when Olivia called.

She called him three times on his cell before he made it to his apartment. She left a message on his voicemail on the last attempt. When he got home, he took off his suit and ceremoniously placed it in its garment bag, then hung it up in his closet. His home phone rang a short while later.

"You got a lot of nerve," he said before the person on the other end could get a word out.

"Saint," Josephine purred.

"There was no reason for you to call Marion Claude and tell him about me."

"I did you a favor."

"What?"

"Petrescu wanted some payback. It seems he can't let Glenn walk around unpunished for what he did to him five years ago. He'd convinced Claude to arrange an 'attempted robbery' on your beloved friend where both his hands were to be broken."

Saint didn't say a word.

"You know I'm telling you the truth, my love. I've never lied to you, and I never will. When Marion found out how you 'slipped' past his security, not only did he arrange to have the head of his security fired, but he had both his hands broken."

"If what you're saying is true, you can't hold that over my head. I owe you nothing."

"All I want from you is what we agreed upon. Saint is dead. Are we clear?"

"Crystal."

Chapter 6

"Fuck you, fuck you, fuck you, and fuck you," Olivia said, pointing to each of her brothers.

"Olivia, don't play yourself," Jon-Jon said.

"Play myself? No, Jon-Jon. Because of all of you, all I can do is play *with* myself."

"Oh God, sis," David, the oldest of the brothers, said, twisting his face in disgust. "We don't need to hear that."

"Oh no, you're going to hear it. That's why I called this meeting." She pointed to her second oldest brother. "Shawn, you've been happily married for what, seven years?"

"Yeah."

"And you, David. You're married and have two kids with Toya. Mike, you're not married to Mia, but you two have been together for years. Even Jon-Jon's nasty ass has a girlfriend. All of you have someone. I've never, ever butted into your relationships."

"We're different, Olivia—" Mike started to say.

"Different my ass."

"We don't have shit," Jon-Jon said. "So, the women we're with can't get shit. If a nigga gets with you and decides he wants a divorce, he's taking half our shit."

"*Our* shit? I just heard you say you didn't have shit," Olivia said.

"I'm talking about the business."

"You're talking about *my* business."

"It's like that?" David asked.

"Yeah, it's like that. Everyone here has their life. Butta Cutz is mine. I appreciate the way y'all regulate, making sure dudes don't come in here and try to play themselves, but y'all can't regulate my personal life. Not anymore. Clayton is a good man."

"I don't like him," Mike snorted.

"Me neither," Jon-Jon chimed in.

"Don't you get it? I don't give a fuck who you like and don't like. It stops today. My personal life is off limits. I'll see who I want to see. Are we clear on that?"

None of them responded.

"I said are we clear?" She slammed her fists on her desk and shot out of her chair.

"Yo, what the fuck?" Jon-Jon said, startled.

"All right, sis," David said. "We got that. Your personal life is off limits. Just calm down before you pop a blood vessel."

"Word," Shawn said. "You said fuck like a hundred times."

Olivia flopped back down into her chair. "Get the hell out of my office."

The brothers looked at each other for a minute. Then, one by one, they got up and left.

Olivia leaned back in her chair, closed her eyes, tilted her head to the side, and massaged her neck. Her massage didn't come close to Saint's. She cut her eyes at her phone. With a sigh, she leaned forward and picked it up. She dialed his number, praying he would answer. On the tenth ring, she hung up and cursed Mike. Her blood pressure almost shot through the roof the previous day when he came strutting back into Butta Cutz and told her, "Mr. Clayton Andrews won't be showing his pretty face around here anymore." She wanted to be mad at Clayton, but she couldn't. How he was reacting was typical for a lot of men who met her brothers.

She picked up her phone and dialed one more number.

"Hello."

"Glenn, it's Olivia."

"Hi, how you doing?"

"I'm doing great. Miki couldn't wait to show me the big article they ran in the *Daily News* this morning. It's on page three."

"I got to pick it up and read it when I get a chance."

"Do me a favor when you get a chance."

"Anything."

"Tell your friend if he doesn't want to see me, be a man and tell me to my face."

"Olivia—"

"Just give him that message for me, will you?"

"Of course."

Olivia hung up. A moment later, line one on her phone lit up.

"What's up, Miki?"

"We got a walk-in. He insists that only you can cut his hair."

"What's his name?"

"Byron Turner."

Olivia dropped her head. "Have Chuck sit him in my chair. I'll be out in a minute."

"Gotcha."

As she neared her chair, she heard Byron shooting some weak game at Lynise, to which she politely smiled. His attention quickly turned to Olivia when he saw her coming his way.

"Hey, you," he said, getting out of the chair to shake her hand. "Congratulations on making this morning's paper."

"Thank you."

"I made some calls to my buddies in California, Philly, Detroit, and Washington. They're in."

"In for what?"

"What I've been trying to tell you all along. Making Butta Cutz a franchise. In ten years, we can have a Butta Cutz in all the major cities."

"Why would you make all these calls and deals without first consulting me? All you did was waste your time."

"Wait, Olivia—"

"No, Byron. We're going to get something straight right now. We're not doing business together, and we are never going to do business together."

"It's like that?"

"And then some."

"Well, can you at least discuss it with you husband?"

She flashed him a stink smile. "I consult with no one, and all of my decisions are final. Now, if you'll excuse me." Olivia walked away.

"What about my haircut?"

"Lynise will take care of you, won't you, Lynise?"

"Yes, Miss Martin."

"Baby!"

"Yeah, ma."

"Caffeine, please."

"Gotcha, ma."

Saint had just pulled into the parking lot of the Adult Learning Center when his cell phone vibrated.

"What's up, Glenn?"

"How do you sleep at night?"

"Very well, thanks for asking."

"Olivia just called me. She told me to give you a message."

"What is it?"

"Be a man and tell her to her face that it's over."

"Over? There wasn't anything between us."

"You lie like a rug."

"I got to go, Glenn."

"Seriously, Saint. If this is how you're going to play it, at least respect her enough to tell her to her face."

"Talk to you later, Glenn."

Saint stood in front of Butta Cutz. After hanging up with Glenn, he knew he was right. She deserved an explanation, even if it was going to be a lie. He ended class at two o'clock and then headed to his apartment to change into an accountant-appropriate suit.

Miki was at the reception desk leafing through an issue of *Vibe Magazine* when he walked in. She looked up from the article she was reading and flashed him an I-want-to-eat-you-alive grin.

"Hi, Miki, how are you doing?" he asked, approaching the desk.

"Fantabulous."

"Is Olivia around?"

Miki looked up. "She's upstairs. Said she doesn't want to be disturbed."

"I really need to speak with her."

"She's like supermangry right now."

"Super what?"

"Super mad angry. And I think it's got something to do with you."

"Think so?"

"She drew a picture of your face."

"What does that mean?" Saint inquired.

"She draws pictures of people when they piss her off. Then she tapes them to her heavy bag, and she...you know." Miki threw a couple jabs.

"Are you serious?"

"You might want to come back tomorrow."

"Miki, I really need to see her now."

Miki looked up toward the ceiling, imagining the work Olivia was putting in on that heavy bag, and shuddered.

"Esther, cover me for a minute."

"Sure, no problem."

Miki walked from behind the receptionist desk with a key in her hand. "When we get up there, make sure you stand in front of me. She's got a wicked left hook, and I'm not trying to get caught with one of them."

Saint followed her outside to the entrance of the apartments above the salon. Miki unlocked the door and looked back at Saint before heading up.

Saint remembered Olivia telling him that she owned the apartments above the salon, but he didn't know she lived in one of them.

Miki stopped at one of the apartment doors and listened before knocking. She could hear combinations of thumps echoing off the heavy bag. She knocked on the door and then took a step back. The thumping stopped.

Saint could hear bare feet heading toward the door right before it swung open.

"Miki, didn't I tell you—" Olivia stopped in mid sentence when her eyes landed on Saint. She blinked as if seeing a mirage.

Saint blinked, as well. Olivia was wearing powder blue sweats with a matching sports bra. Her hair was pulled back into a ponytail and she was dripping sweat.

"I know what you said, but Clayton said he really had to speak to you." Miki looked to him for help.

"Can we talk?" he asked.

Olivia patted herself dry with the towel around her neck and walked away from the door.

"Thank you, Miki," Saint said.

"Don't thank me. I think I just led you to the lion's den."

Saint walked in and closed the door. He immediately noticed that the apartment was actually two. Olivia had the connecting wall knocked down, and the two apartments were converted into one big studio. In the corner, there was a Bow Flex machine and a treadmill. In the center of the room, suspended from a chain bolted to the central beam, was a heavy bag. On the other side of the room, Olivia retrieved a bottle of water from the refrigerator and slammed the door.

"I didn't know you lived here above the salon," he said.

"I don't," Olivia responded, walking to the heavy bag and ripping a piece of paper off of it. "Say what you came to say so you can leave and I can get back to my workout."

Olivia put her boxing gloves back on and stood staring at him with her hands on her hips.

Saint walked up to her. The heat radiating from her made his temperature rise. And her scent. *Her* scent, the one that would forever remind him of droplets before a hard rain, was suffocating his thoughts. He watched a bead of sweat run from her temple, down her cheek, down the side of her neck as if caressing it, and then end its course between her cleavage.

His eyes instinctively closed as a blur entered his peripheral vision. He staggered to his right when Olivia's wicked left hook caught him on the side of the head.

"That's for playing with my head," she said.

Saint held his head in shock. "Olivia—"

Her right jab landed square on his chin, causing him to stagger backwards.

"And that's for not being man enough to stand up to my brothers."

"Olivia, hold up," Saint said, holding his hands out in front of himself. "I'm not going to let you hit me again."

She feinted like she was going to hit him, and he backpedaled.

"Say what you got to say and then leave," Olivia said, approaching him. "Or are you not man enough to tell me to my face?"

"Stop walking toward me like that."

"Like what?" Olivia threw a punch at him, which he dodged.

"You know what?" he said, loosening his tie.

"What are you doing?" Olivia asked, cocking her head. "Are you growing a pair of balls?"

Saint took off his suit jacket and rolled up his sleeves. "This is what you want? You want to fight? Let's fight. Get it out of your system. Give me a pair of gloves."

Olivia took off her gloves.

"What are you doing?"

"What does it look like I'm doing?"

"All right, Olivia. I'm serious now, all jokes aside."

Olivia's eyes were brimming with tears. "How could I be so naïve? All the men who hit on me, I can see it from a mile away."

"Olivia—"

"Fuck you, Clayton!" she yelled, then charged at him.

Olivia's movement was lightening quick, but for Saint, it was snail slow. He watched her as she came in low, a common kickboxing feint. He could tell she trained well, but she would learn in a second that the well trained could never beat the well experienced. He had played her next three moves in his head. She was positioning herself to execute a spinning roundhouse kick to his sternum. He would step to her right, causing her to most likely follow through with a straight right jab to his face. He would then stumble to her left. Thinking him to be off balance, she would come with her wicked left hook.

His eyes got bigger as the beginning of her spin commenced. Like a well-choreographed dance, Saint led and she followed.

Olivia's kick missed; Saint stood in line with her hand. She let it go. Her punch grazed his cheek; he stumbled to her left. She smiled as her left hook, perfectly executed, headed for his chin. One second, his chin was there, and then it wasn't. She missed and was off balance. Saint had disappeared. She gasped as she felt his arms clamp down around her from behind. She struggled against his crushing bear hug, but with her arms pinned to her sides, there wasn't much she could do but thrash about in his grip.

"Get off of me!" she yelled.

He spun her around, and before she could gather her wits, she was off her feet and pinned against the wall. Saint watched her chest heave as she struggled against his death grip. He locked eyes with her and then smashed his mouth against hers.

A moan escaped Olivia's mouth as Saint's tongue grazed hers. She opened her mouth wider, allowing his tongue to explore deeper. She tongue wrestled with him as he slowly dry humped her. She imagined his hardness splitting her open, stretching her walls, filling her to maximum capacity. Then she bit down on his tongue.

"Ah," Saint mumbled.

"Put me down," Olivia muttered.

"Um, all right, all right." Saint allowed her to slide down the wall until her feet touched the floor.

She shoved him back. "I'm through with you, Clayton."

"Olivia, wait—"

"I refuse to let you play me like some puppet. I want you out of my apartment and out of my life."

Saint walked over to where he had dropped his tie and suit jacket and picked them up. Without looking back, he walked to the door, but as his hand rested on the knob, he took one last look at her from over his shoulder.

"In another lifetime, we would be the perfect couple."

Olivia jumped when Saint closed the door behind himself. She slid down the wall and hung her head as the tears freely fell from her eyes. She cried until her eyes were bloodshot red. Afterwards, she slowly got to her feet and went to the sink where she splashed water on her face and pulled herself together. She had to keep reminding herself that she was a strong woman and that Clayton was only a man. He wasn't the first man to hurt her, and he wouldn't be the last.

Marion Claude's visit gave Olivia worldwide recognition. Her volume of customers swelled so much that she let Jon-Jon talk her into hiring two of Lynise's friends.

Byron became a regular customer. He even convinced a few of his partners to become regulars, as well. As usual, Butta Cutz blessed everyone with happiness except Olivia.

In Kew Gardens, Saint sat in his apartment grading papers and thinking of Olivia. Glenn tried convincing him to come to Butta Cutz with him, but as bad as he wanted Olivia in his life, he knew he could never be the man she needed him to be. As long as Josephine had his soul, he could never give Olivia his heart.

He took off his glasses and rubbed his eyes. "Josephine," he whispered. He dedicated his life to her, body and soul, building her an empire off of the blood and fear of her rivals. There wasn't a continent where Josephine Delacroix wasn't respected. She was a shrewd businesswoman who wouldn't think twice about invoking the wrath of The Saint upon anyone who dared oppose her. Anyone who knew of The Saint knew he didn't just kill; he taunted. He would first kill any pets one had, and then he would take out their bodyguards one by one. At that point, they would be breaking their necks trying to get in touch with Josephine to call him off. One would die a thousand deaths before he delivered the lethal blow.

Saint examined his hands. Calloused and conditioned. He imagined his heart being the same way. It had to be. That was probably the only reason why that dagger hadn't penetrated it. The doctors couldn't explain it. A medical miracle was what they called it.

That was the opportune time to kill Josephine, rid himself of her forever. She was the one who sent *HER* to assassinate him. But, Josephine had come to his hospital bed, crying and begging for his forgiveness. She said she didn't realize how much she had truly loved him until she found out she nearly lost him. Saint forgave her on one condition. That she would let him go. That she would allow him to go anywhere in the world he chose and live a normal life. She agreed, but with two conditions of her own. His whereabouts would only be known to her and he would never side with her enemies.

He thought of Laurent Petrescu, a bookkeeper for the Rumanian mob masquerading as a tailor/fashion designer and traveling the world to keep an eye on their investments. Then there was Marion Claude, a designer of fashion, but not the type you could wear to a family picnic. His line of fashion consisted of body armored suits outfitted with numerous concealed pockets for weaponry. Although Saint was out of "the business" as everyone called it, he still kept up on who was who. Information was power.

He yawned, stretching his arms out wide. He looked at the papers he hadn't graded yet and decided tomorrow was another day.

"Sure is lonely, huh?" he said to himself.

"Yeah, lonely but peaceful."

"I wonder what Olivia is doing right now."

"I don't care."

"Yes, you do."

"Yeah…I do."

"I say we gear up and—"

"I say I stop talking to myself and go to bed."

"Whatever you say. You're the boss."

Chapter 7

Olivia sat in her office with her eyes closed as she listened to her morning messages. Most were calling to congratulate her on her upcoming appearance on *Oprah*. She'd been receiving many phone calls from talk shows after Marion Claude came through, but she turned them all down. It was Baby, Esther, Grace, and her brothers who convinced her to go on *Oprah*. They told her that if she didn't, they would disown her.

Business was booming. So much so that she took Byron up on his offer. It was time for Butta Cutz to go nationwide.

Just as the last message ended, Miki called her on line one.

"What's up, Miki?"

"Your nine-thirty is here."

"Tell Mr. Ryan that I'll be out in a minute."

She finished her double Espresso and slipped on her shoes.

"Okay, now. There she is," Mr. Ryan said, getting out of Olivia's barber chair and bowing his head.

"Cut it out, old man." Olivia hugged him and kissed him on the cheek.

He was one of the few who remembered Butta Cutz when it was just Brady's Barbershop. For as long as she could remember, Mr. Ryan would come in every Saturday, and Brady would hook him up with a Caesar and a shave. Olivia kept the tradition going, and just like old man Brady, she never charged him. The way he kept her laughing as she hooked him up was payment enough.

"So what will it be?" she asked with a smile.

"Girl, don't play wit' me. I been coming in this here place from since before you was born, and I always gets me a Caesar and a shave wit' the straight razor."

"You sure I can't interest you in a pedicure? Baby will do you up real special. Right, Baby?"

"Oh yeah, I can't wait to get my hands on those feet," Baby teased.

"Yous a keep on waiting, 'cause you or nobody else is getting near these dogs."

Everyone started cracking up.

"C'mon, Mr. Ryan," Olivia teased on, "all men are getting their toes done these days."

"Back in my day, we had a name for men like that."

"What's that, Mr. Ryan?" Esther asked from her barber chair.

"Homosexuals."

"Ooohhh, nooooo," everybody said in unison.

Olivia swatted him on the shoulder. "Just because a man gets his toes done doesn't mean he's a homosexual, Mr. Ryan."

"He's just taking pride in his appearance," Chuck added.

Ryan turned his neck to face him. "Didn't you tell me the other day that you was a homosexual?"

"I said metrosexual."

"That ain't nothing but a new word y'all done came up with to hide what you is."

"Ain't nothing homo about me," Chuck said, flexing his pecs behind his tank top.

"Ooohhh weeeee," Esther, Miki, and Olivia said.

"You ain't did nothing slick, Slick," Mr. Ryan said, starting to unbutton his shirt.

Olivia draped her chair cloth over him, stopping him. "Calm down, old man. These young bucks don't know what time it is."

"Homosexual, metrosexual, DL brothers," Mr. Ryan grumbled.

"What you know about DL brothers?" Esther asked, keeping the conversation going.

"I know to stay the hell away from them."

"How you know who they are if they on the DL?" Baby asked.

"You got to look for the signs," Mr. Ryan replied, placing emphasis on the word "signs".

"What are the signs?" Esther pressed.

"When your man's earrings hang lower than yours, your antennas better go up. If he wears spandex and tweezes his eyebrows, watch out. If y'all be having arguments over him being in the mirror longer than you or he's always admiring himself in the mirror, he is definitely a DL brother."

"You're too much," Olivia said.

"He ain't lying, though," Baby said.

"What you know about DL brothers?" Olivia asked.

"Remember Johnny?"

"The guy you were all in love with last summer?"

"Yeah. He was a DL brother," Baby informed them.

"Get out of here!" Miki said, walking up on the conversation.

"I saw the signs, but I refused to believe it. Mr. Ryan ain't lying, especially the part about being in the mirror longer than me. That was the first sign. But, when he asked me to do some freaky shit one night, I two-pieced him."

"What did he ask you to do?" Miki asked, her eyes wide.

"All I'm going to say is he wanted me to put my thumb where it didn't have no business being."

"And you two-pieced him?" Miki asked, astonished.

"Shit, I was going to four-piece him, but the two-piece put him out cold."

"Damn, Baby," said the young gentleman getting a pedicure by Lynise. "Tell me what I got to do to get you on my team."

"After that episode, I'm a free agent, no commitments. And anybody who wants to get with me, his paper got to be the way I like my dicks: long and strong."

"Baby!" Olivia yelled over the roars and claps.

She didn't mind a little trash talking as long as the language wasn't too graphic.

"And why the hell are you so quiet?" Chuck asked Grace, who looked like she was about to burst.

"Glenn wanted me to wait until he got here, but…" She paused and looked at Olivia. "He proposed to me last night."

"And?" Baby asked.

"And I said yes!" Grace started jumping up and down.

Baby, Esther, Miki, and Olivia ran to her and crowded around her for a group hug.

"My girl is getting married," Olivia said.

"And I'm getting old," Mr. Ryan commented.

"Oh, hush up. My girl is getting married."

The women talked for a couple minutes before getting back to work.

Byron walked in, strutting like he was walking down a runway. Mr. Ryan elbowed Olivia and mouthed, *DL*. She started laughing.

"Olivia, how are you?" Byron asked.

"I'm fine. How 'bout yourself?"

"Wonderful." He looked at his watch and then looked at Lynise. "Am I early?"

"No, I'll be with you in a second."

"No rush. I'll be in the boardroom."

"I think he likes you," Baby said. "He won't allow anyone to touch his head, hands, or feet but you."

Lynise smiled bashfully. Olivia was just glad he had stopped sweating her.

Everyone froze when Glenn walked through the door.

"You told them," he said to Grace.

"Congratulations!" everyone shouted.

Grace ran into his arms. "I'm sorry, baby. I tried to hold it, but they dragged it out of me."

"Yeah," Baby said, "we had to twist her arm."

Grace stuck up her middle finger at her.

Forty minutes later, Olivia was just finishing off Mr. Ryan, when her oldest brother David walked in.

"What brings you around here?" she asked.

"I need a reason to come see my little sister?"

"What's wrong? Toya okay?"

"Everything's fine. I was in the neighborhood and decided to drop in to see how you were doing."

"Other than working twelve hours a day and having appointments booked as far ahead as next year, I'm doing just great."

"That's wonderful."

"Why don't you go wait in my office? I'll be there in a minute."

"Sure."

Olivia walked in fifteen minutes later.

"Okay, what's the real deal?"

"Sis, everything is fine. I'm just dropping by."

Olivia folded her arms and stared at him for a minute before walking to her chair and sitting down. "You'll have to excuse me. I'm just not used to you coming here just to see how I'm doing."

"Well, get used to it. Me, Jon-Jon, Shawn, and Mike had a meeting after we all had our meeting the other day."

"Oh really?"

"Yeah, we kinda agreed that we've been a little too over-protective with you."

"You think?"

"You got to understand—"

Olivia held her hand up. "I understand. The business, dudes trying to get with me just to get a piece of Butta Cutz."

"It's more than that." David sat on the edge of the chair. "You were young when mom died, but do you remember how close we all were?"

Olivia nodded.

"She was beautiful, inside and out."

Olivia put her head down.

"The night she died was like any other night in our household. We would eat dinner, take our showers, brush our teeth, and go to bed. No one saw it coming. Just like that, she died in her sleep." David's eyes were brimming with tears. "You and mom could pass for twins."

Olivia dabbed at her tears as they ran down her cheeks.

David continued. "She just slipped through our hands. She was the glue that held us together. Then you became that glue. If anything was to happen to you, me, Jon-Jon, Shawn and Mike would lose our minds. So, we hover over you, not because we don't want you to have a personal life. We just know how it feels to have the woman of our lives snatched from us, and we're not trying to lose anymore women in our family."

"I don't know what to say."

"You don't have to say anything. Just know that we love you and see you as the mother hen. And we're not going to let anything happen to you."

"I appreciate everything you guys do for me. You know I wouldn't be where I am today if it wasn't for y'all. I still say y'all should be with me when I go on *Oprah*."

"No, that's your time to shine. And you *are* going to shine."

Olivia stood up and hugged her brother.

"So how are you and the accountant doing?"

"We broke up."

"You're joking, right?"

"Nope. I think he has some unresolved issues in his life that he has to find closure with."

"That's what he told you?"

"No, that's what Dr. Phil would've said."

"Oh, God. You and Dr. Phil."

"The man is a psychological genius."

"Well, I'm not a psychological genius, but I know you. And I know you were feeling some kind a way about that guy.

Maybe you should use your 'Dr. Phil' skills and help him resolve his issues."

"I got bigger things to worry about right now. Byron secured a store front in Queens on Merrick Boulevard."

David nodded. "Okay, we doing big things. A Butta Cutz in Queens. I'm feeling that."

"And I talked to his man in Philly. He's ready to convert his barbershop into a Butta Cutz."

"Ummm."

"And…Grace is getting married."

"Get out of here!"

"Glenn proposed to her last night."

David just smiled.

"What?" Olivia asked.

"It's good to see you happy."

"I am. And I'm going to treat myself."

"Not another pair of shoes."

"No, butthead. I'm going to go home, curl up on my couch, and break night watching the *Law & Order* marathon."

"You're playing, right?"

"Heck no. I'm staying up all night and then I'm taking tomorrow off."

"Well, I guess it's better than getting another pair of shoes."

Olivia punched him in the arm.

Olivia jumped out of her sleep when she heard the pounding on her front door. She looked at her clock; it was ten in the morning. As planned, she broke night watching *Law & Order* and had just drifted off to sleep. She grabbed her robe and rushed to the door thinking it was one of her brothers.

"Hold on," she said as she slid the bolt off.

She stepped back in shock when she opened the door.

"You're through!" Byron shouted, spittle flying out his mouth. He threw a 9x12 manila envelope at her. "You think you can play me, bitch? I'm going to show you how to play the game. When I'm done suing you, you're going to be selling *your* ass. I'm closing your whorehouse down."

"What are you talking about?"

Byron lifted his hand as if he was going to smack her.

"See you in court." He spat at her feet, marched to his car, and filled the early morning with screeching tires as he pulled off.

Olivia looked at the envelope that she realized she was clutching to her chest. She opened it and pulled out the piece of paper balled up inside. In big letters, Byron had written *FUCK YOU*. As she read the letter, her hands started shaking. She pulled out the pictures and looked at them one by one. Each made her madder than the last. She threw them against the wall, then sat in the middle of the floor and cried.

Olivia's grief quickly turned to scorching anger. She ran to her room and threw on a pair of jeans, a sweater, and a pair of sneakers. She snatched her car keys up and ran out her house, leaving the front door wide open. She realized in her rush to get to the salon that she didn't have her driver's license on her, so she slowed down to the speed limit. She couldn't afford getting pulled over. Not now. She had some work to put in. Once her car came to a screeching halt, she jumped out without turning off the engine.

Miki's eyes lit up when she saw Olivia walk in. Her mouth dropped open when she saw the dark look on her face. Olivia scanned the salon until she spotted the dead man walking. The whole scene unfolded in slow motion as Olivia ran up on Lynise and delivered her wicked left hook to the side of Lynise's temple. She collapsed like a beach chair. Olivia kicked her motionless body three times before remembering she had two more victims. She looked up like a rabid dog and her eyes locked with Lynise's two friends who Jon-Jon had convinced her to hire, Renee and Simone.

Renee backed up and was about to run for the front door, but Baby grabbed her by her long weave and used her face as a punching bag. She didn't know what Lynise and her friends had done, but seeing Olivia ready to catch a body had her ready to be her co-defendant. Esther, Grace, and Miki were all on the same page. Esther started after Simone, who was now scrambling toward the front door. Grace stood in front of it like a raging bull ready to charge. Miki came flying from behind the reception desk with a bat. Chuck ushered the customers out and locked the door as Jordan tried to break up the simultaneous fights. When Chuck turned around, Olivia was on top of Simone pounding her face in like a meat tenderizer. Baby and Esther had tag-teamed Renee. Miki stood in the center of it all gripping the bat, thirsty to bash somebody's head in.

Lynise made the fatal mistake of coming to and trying to get to her feet. Miki's face twisted into a mask of anger as she swung the bat at Lynise's head. God must've been on Lynise's side, because she twisted her ankle as she tried to get up and fell. The bat skinned the top of her head, causing her to gasp.

One of the customers must've seen Jon-Jon on their way down the block and told him what was happening, because he was at the door fumbling with his key to open it. He finally got in.

"Olivia! What the fuck is going on?"

Hearing his voice made her look up. Her fingers curled into claws as she stormed toward him. Miki blinked as Olivia snatched the bat out of her hands.

"I trusted you," Olivia cried out like a wounded animal.

Jon-Jon walked toward her, acting like he was mad, as well. "Put that fucking bat down."

"You bastard!" Olivia swung the bat, cracking him square on the shoulder.

Jon-Jon backed up in shock.

Olivia swung the bat again. This time, he didn't call her bluff. He backpedaled and ran out the salon.

"Get these bitches in the back before I kill them," she told Chuck and Jordan through clenched teeth.

"Baby!" Olivia screamed. "That's enough."

Although Lynise had blacked out long ago, Baby was still banging her limp head against her barber chair.

Baby looked up at Olivia to make sure she was all right and then smashed Lynise's head against the chair one last time before letting her drop to the floor.

Chuck and Jordan helped Renee and Simone to their feet and walked them to the back.

"Y'all bitches is lucky you ain't dead," Jordan said.

When Chuck returned to the front, he smacked Lynise a couple times. "Boss, I think she may need an ambulance."

"Move!" Baby said, sizing her up like a punter about to kick the shit out of a football. "I'll wake her ass up."

Olivia grabbed Baby by one of her suspenders. "Back off, Baby."

Everyone looked outside when they saw the flashing lights of a police car.

"Shit!" Olivia said, then sighed with relief when she saw it was her brother and his partner.

"Olivia, what's going on?" he asked, ready to put some work in himself.

"I'm going to kill Jon-Jon."

"Jon-Jon did this?"

"He's the cause of it."

Mike got on his radio. "79 to base. Situation all clear."

"Copy that," the dispatcher said.

"Chuck, you and Jordan take her to the back," Olivia said, pointing to Lynise.

Mike watched as the two men lifted her up and carried her to the back. His partner looked at him. He shot his partner the don't-worry-it's-okay look.

"Why don't you go wait in the car, Gee? I got this."

"Whatever you say, Mike."

"Sis, you need to tell me from the beginning what happened."

Olivia walked to the front door, locked it, and flipped the sign from Open to Closed. Everyone followed her to the back where she nudged Lynise until she came to. Then they all sat down and listened in shock as Lynise told them how Jon-Jon came up with the idea to run an escort service from her shop. She, Renee, and Simone propositioned certain wealthy clients, the ones who they knew wouldn't tell what they were doing.

Those who wanted the "complete package" would call Jon-Jon and tell him ahead of time. He would then set up the apartment that Olivia let him stay in from time to time above the salon. Once that certain client got their haircut, manicure, or pedicure, Jon-Jon would lead them to the apartment where Lynise, Renee, or Simone would be waiting.

Lynise, Renee, and Simone all swore, as God be their witness, that they weren't going to press charges or say anything to anyone. The one truth they did tell from the start was being students at Hunter College. They knew if this got out, they would no longer be allowed to attend. Everyone parted the way and let them walk out on their own two feet.

After they left, Olivia shared with everyone the visit that Byron had paid her, and she told them about the extortion note and pictures. Jon-Jon had taken pictures of Lynise, Renee, and Simone "servicing" Bryon on different occasions. Jon-Jon was trying to sell the pictures to him.

"All my years of hard work were for nothing." Olivia said, on the verge of crying.

"I'll go have a chat with Byron," Mike said.

"No, that's exactly what he would want," Olivia told him.

"What *does* he want?" Glenn asked.

"He wants to sue me and make a public spectacle of me."

"There has to be a way to reason with him," Grace said.

"The way he was talking earlier, I don't know if he's open to any kind of reasoning."

"Maybe when he cools off," Miki said, hoping to lighten the mood.

Olivia shook her head. "No matter how you look at it, he's going to fuck me, whether he sues me or if he wants to deal. I would have to basically accept any deal he shoves in my face." Olivia turned to her brother so fast he jumped. "You tell Jon-Jon to do himself a favor and don't come anywhere near me. I swear I will hurt that boy."

Glenn stood up. "I gotta run."

"Run?" Grace said. "Now?"

"Yeah, I have a lunch appointment with—"

"Cancel it. We need you here."

"No," Olivia said. "Go handle your business, Glenn."

"I'll be back at seven to pick you up," he said to Grace.

She acted like she didn't hear him.

Mike walked Glenn to the front door and let him out. As soon as Glenn's feet hit the curb, he flipped open his cell and hit the speed dial.

"We need to talk. Shit has hit the fan."

"Yeah, Glenn, you can tell me all about it tomorrow," Saint sighed.

"There might not be a tomorrow for Butta Cutz."

Chapter 8

For the past two days, Jon-Jon had been staying with his man Ira. His brothers were blowing his cell phone up, leaving all kinds of messages for him to get in touch with them as soon as possible. Jon-Jon wasn't up to facing them or Olivia. He'd fucked up.

I should've stayed with the white motherfuckers, he thought to himself. *They just coughed the money up. It's always a black motherfucker that got to throw a monkey wrench in the program and fuck shit up.*

Jon-Jon took one more drag off his cigarette before flicking it onto the sidewalk and heading into Ira's apartment building. Although Ira worked the midnight shift and wouldn't be home right now, Jon-Jon still respected his "no smoking" rule.

On his way up the stairs, his cell rang. He looked at the caller ID. He didn't recognize the number, which meant it was probably one of his brothers calling from someone else's phone. He tucked his cell back in his jacket and pulled out the apartment keys. He knew he couldn't avoid the family forever.

He just needed some time to think on how he was going to take care of Mr. Byron Turner.

He unlocked the door and stepped inside. The apartment was in total darkness, which wasn't unusual. It was just after midnight, and Ira always turned off all the lights when he left for work. What was unusual was when he hit the light switch and nothing happened.

"You're a hard man to track down," a voice said in the darkness.

Jon-Jon reached for his gun. He felt it snatched out of his waistband a fraction of a second before his hand got there, causing him to grab nothing but air. He threw a punch at the figure in front of him. The figure moved like a phantom.

Jon-Jon gasped as a hand wrapped around his neck and the other pinned him against the wall. The figure's face came into view when he stepped into the light coming through the window from the street lamp.

When Jon-Jon saw his face, he started struggling. There was no way he would let a nerd-ass, bean counter rough him up.

Saint took a step back and threw a straight jab to the right side of Jon-Jon's chest, just inside his right shoulder. Jon-Jon stumbled sideways from the impact. The pain was so intense that he stopped breathing.

"You fucked up one time this week. Let's not make it twice. Give me the disks with the pictures of all the clients you've been setting up."

"I don't know what you're talking about."

Saint delivered another knockout blow, this one aimed at the same point on his left side.

"My arms!" Jon-Jon screamed, panicking. "I can't feel my arms!"

"Waste any more of my time and you won't feel your legs either."

"Who are you? You ain't no accountant."

"Disks, where are they?" Saint swept Jon-Jon's feet from under him. When he fell flat on his ass, Saint rested his heel on Jon-Jon's leg socket.

"Okay, okay. In the back room…in the Timberland box."

Saint dragged him to the room and shoved him into the corner. He saw the box next to the bed. He picked it up, carried it to the desk, and opened Jon-Jon's laptop. He checked both disks and nodded.

"These are the originals?"

Jon-Jon nodded.

"And you don't have any more?"

Jon-Jon shook his head. "That's it."

"Three things," Saint said as he prepared to leave. "I'm going to clean up the mess you got your sister in. So, if you got any stupid ideas of doing anything to Byron, forget about it. Number two, if I find out you're lying to me, I will paralyze you permanently. And number three, get your life together."

Saint stuffed the disks in his jacket and took off just as silently as he came.

"Jerry," Byron said to the guy on the other end of his cell phone, "trust me on this one. This investment with Double Platinum Records is going to pay you triple what you're putting in."

Byron walked into the office building in Long Island City, where his office was located on the fifth floor.

"Have I ever failed you before? You damn right I never have, and I'm not going to start now."

He pressed the elevator button. Five minutes later, he was on his floor working on another deal on his cell phone. He stopped in his tracks.

"I'm going to have to call you back," he said before hanging up, then looked at his secretary like he was going to fire her.

"Mr. Turner—"

Byron quickly cut her off with a huff. "What are you doing here?" he asked Olivia.

"You're not returning my phone calls; your secretary refuses to tell me when you're in. It's like you're avoiding me."

"It's not *like* I'm avoiding you. I am. Anything you have to say, tell it to your lawyer and have him relay it to mine."

He spun on her and headed to his office.

"Byron…please," Olivia called after him.

He turned and looked at her like she was an annoying gnat. Then he looked at his secretary. "Hold all my calls. Miss Martin and I have some business to discuss."

"Yes, Mr. Turner."

Byron cut his eyes at Olivia and walked toward his office. Olivia followed him in and started to sit down, but he stopped her.

"Don't. You're not going to be here for long."

Olivia folded her arms and stared at him, as he folded his and slowly circled her.

"All I wanted to do was work with you, make us a lot of money. That's what I do. I make plenty money."

"Byron—"

"Shut…the fuck…up!" he snapped. "You're in my world now. You have no say. All you do is listen, and if you want any kind of life, you will do exactly as I say. Am I clear?"

Olivia was so hot with anger that her face was glowing.

"I'm listening."

Byron stopped circling her and placed his hands behind his back as he dramatically walked to his office window and looked out. Without looking back at her, he spoke.

"What did you think you could gain by trying to blackmail me?"

"I had no idea that was going on."

"The girls work at your salon, fuck clients in your apartments, and you had no idea it was going on?"

"I'm sitting on a goldmine, Byron. You know that. The last thing I would want to do is run a prostitution ring out of it."

"What does your husband think about all this?"

Olivia was about to tell him the truth about the whole Clayton situation, but something told her that he would somehow try and use it against her.

"We're not speaking to each other right now."

"Does he know you're here now?"

"No."

"Seems to me that he doesn't care what happens to you."

Olivia didn't say anything.

"Funny thing is, I do." Byron finally turned around to face her. "When I look at you, I see money, and I like money." He walked up on her. "But, I also see someone who tried to *fuck me*, and that…I don't like." He let his eyes freely roam over her before looking into her eyes. "Do you know where Nell's is?"

"It's on 14th Street."

"That's where we'll be eating tomorrow night."

"I'm not going anywhere with you," Olivia said in a seething tone.

"I'll make it real easy for you to understand. I get on the phone, call my people at the *Daily News* and *New York Post*, and they will print whatever I tell them to. Then I call my very close friend who plays golf with the police commissioner. The police will shut your spot down and arrest everyone and charge them with promoting prostitution." He got right up in her face. "The only hair you'll be cutting is the hair off of Big Bertha's back in the prison bath hall."

Olivia took a step back. She tried her best to will her forming tears not to fall, but one did. She quickly turned away from him, but he grabbed her by the chin and made her face him.

"Not so tough after all."

Olivia slapped his hand away and turned to leave.

"Tomorrow night, eight o'clock, and don't keep me waiting."

Olivia stormed out of his office. Her knees were threatening to give out on her, and her stomach was shouting for her to find the nearest bathroom to throw up. Her mind was going in so many directions at once that she didn't see the man standing in her path. She bumped into him, knocking his newspaper to the floor.

"I'm sorry," she said, starting to bend down to pick it up.

The man stopped her. "Don't worry about it, Miss—"

"Martin," Olivia said, looking into his hazel eyes.

The man bent down and picked up his paper. "My name's Dr. Whitman. Pleased to meet you."

He stood about six feet. He wore a three-piece suit, and his shoulder-length dreads came down on each side of his face.

"I'm kind of nervous. Got a big meeting with Mr. Turner," he said sheepishly.

Hearing Byron's name reminded Olivia that she needed to hurry and look for that bathroom. Without another word, she took off.

Dr. Whitman watched her disappear around the corner and then shrugged his shoulders.

"Mr. Turner will see you now, Dr. Whitman," the secretary said, hanging up her phone.

Olivia put her finger in her ears as three of her brothers, Baby, Esther, Grace, Miki, Chuck, and Jordan argued back and forth. The only thing they agreed on was that there wasn't going to be any compromising with Byron. The girls wanted to call up some people that they knew at the newspapers and magazines and run counter articles to whatever Byron may be putting out. The men couldn't decide if they should kill him fast or kill him slow. Mike already paid Lynise, Renee, and Simone a visit. After his long talk with them, there was no one in the universe who could force a confession out of them. What they had done in those apartments would be taken to their graves.

Olivia told them everything that happened with her meeting with Byron. Everything but the date she had with him at eight o'clock that evening. She looked at her watch. It was four-thirty, and they still hadn't come up with a viable solution.

Olivia finally held her hand up. "Enough! We've been going at it since one o'clock. My head is pounding, I'm on the verge of a nervous breakdown, and all this yelling isn't helping."

She got up to leave.

"Where are you going?" Grace asked.

"Home."

"What about this situation?" Mike asked.

"I don't have the strength to continue today. Tomorrow is another day."

"We can't keep putting this off," David said.

Olivia left.

Grace ran up behind her. "Olivia, Glenn made me promise not to tell you, but I can't just sit here and watch you stress like this."

"Promise not to tell me what?"

Grace grabbed her hand and spoke low. "He talked to Clayton."

"Why would he do that?"

"He swore to me that Clayton could make all this go away."

Olivia shook her head. "Grace, I don't need him trying to butt in and make things worse. Call Glenn and tell him that I said to tell Clayton to stay out of this."

"Olivia, what are we going to do?"

"Right now, I'm going home."

Olivia knew she was going to meet Byron, and she knew she wasn't going to let him take advantage of her. What she didn't know was how she was going to stop him from doing that.

After a piping hot shower and a long cry, Olivia began getting ready. She decided to wear a simple dress, nothing tight or insinuating. She'd accepted the fact that Byron may be trying to take everything from her, but the one thing he wasn't going to take was her dignity. She looked at herself one last time in the mirror before leaving.

When she walked into Nell's, she felt her palms getting sweaty. There, in the corner, Byron was sitting at a table running his fingers down the side of his glass. When he saw her, he started smiling like a shark. The closer she got to him, the wider his smile seemed to grow. It was almost as if he was nervous.

"Glad you could make it," he said, pulling out her seat.

Olivia rolled her eyes at him as she sat down. She eyed the extra seat at the table.

"You expecting someone else?"

"You got jokes, huh?" Byron smiled nervously.

Olivia jumped when she felt a pair of strong hands rest on her shoulders.

"Hi, sweetheart," Saint said, kissing her on the cheek. "What I tell you, huh?" he said to Byron as he sat down. "Didn't I tell you she's more punctual than an atomic clock?"

"Byron—" Olivia started to say, but he cut her off.

"Olivia, first, let me just say that the way I handled this whole ordeal was totally out of line."

Olivia blinked to make sure the man sitting in front of her was in fact Byron.

"When I got those pictures and that extortion note, I freaked out. I should've known from our working relationship that you would've never sanctioned anything like that. I would like to humbly apologize for my harsh words and my jumping to conclusions."

"That's it?" she asked in shock. "You were talking about suing and destroying me."

Byron stirred in his seat and smiled nervously at Saint. "Like I said, I was upset. I said those things in the heat of the moment."

Olivia looked at Saint.

He reached into his jacket pocket and pulled out a three-page statement. "See, baby, he even typed up a statement applauding Butta Cutz and its employees, and praising your strict professionalism. And…" Saint reached into his other pocket. "Bryon was kind enough to void all the contracts you signed with him to open up Butta Cutz in different locations."

Olivia snatched the contracts from Saint and inspected them.

"So we're cool, right?" Byron asked, but it was more like a plea.

"I want to know what happened from the time I left your office yesterday until now," Olivia said, putting the contracts on the table.

"Your husband truly cares about you, Olivia. He's shown me that." Byron stood up to leave. "Mr. Andrews," he said, extending his hand.

Saint shook it a little longer than customary.

Byron bowed his head to Olivia and then exited the building like it was on fire.

Olivia stared at Saint. She had forgotten how good he looked. Saint cleared his throat and stood.

"Where are you going?"

"Home."

"Home? You're not going anywhere until you tell me what happened."

"Good night, Olivia."

She followed him outside. "Clayton! Don't walk away from me."

"I'm not walking away from you. You're following me."

She grabbed him by the shoulder and walked in front of him.

"Why would you do this for me after the way we separated?"

"I didn't do it for you. I did it for me."

"For you? What did you get out of it?"

"None of your business."

"You're not an accountant. Who are you really?"

Saint leaned down and whispered in her ear, "If I tell you, I'll have to kill you."

Olivia's mouth dropped. Saint laughed.

"I'm just fucking with you. Go home. Get some sleep."

He walked across the street toward where he parked. He sighed when he heard Olivia running up on him.

"Olivia–" He gasped as he felt her snatch his wallet out of his back pocket. "Hey, what are you doing?"

Olivia opened it and started looking for his identification. Saint made a lazy attempt at snatching it. Olivia backed up. She found his driver's license, Clayton Andrews. Credit cards, Clayton Andrews.

He grabbed her wrist and took his wallet from her, but not before her fingers latched onto a photo ID.

"Clayton Andrews, teacher at the Adult Learning Center." She looked up at him. "What is this?"

Saint snatched it from her.

"You're a teacher?" she asked, following him.

"Yes, I'm a math teacher. I'm not an accountant. I told you that I worked with numbers. You assumed I was an accountant, and I didn't correct your assumption."

"Why?"

"Why do you think?"

"You thought I wouldn't be interested in a math teacher?"

"Would you?"

"Hell no, but after being with you..." She inched closer to him.

Saint stopped her in her tracks. "My life...it's very complicated."

"You're a school teacher. How complicated can it be?"

He put his head down.

"It's Josephine, isn't it?" She could see him tense up at the mention of her name. "The first time I mentioned her name to you, you turned rigid. Do you still love her?"

"Yes," Saint whispered. "She…we have a bond neither one of us could ever walk away from."

Olivia put her head down.

Saint placed his hand on her chin and picked her head up. "I feel like God created you just for me, but…" His words got stuck in his throat.

Olivia allowed her hands to rest on his. "I still owe you a haircut."

"Yes, you do." Saint caressed her face before turning to leave.

"So you're not going to tell me what you did to Byron?"

A sinister smile crept across his face. "All I did was let him know that nobody threatens my wife and gets away with it."

Saint took one more look at her before climbing into his car and driving off. *Damn, she looked so good.* It took every ounce of his discipline not to take her in his arms and kiss her passionately. He looked at himself in the rearview mirror and smiled. He had told the truth again. She now knew he was a math teacher, *and* she was still willing to get with him. But, where was all this truth telling getting him? He still couldn't get with her.

"That's fucked up," he said out loud with a chuckle. "Love is supposed to bring people closer together. When *you* love someone, you have to push them away."

"I don't love her. I don't know her like that."

"You're talking to yourself, remember? So, I know how you feel about her."

"Never could lie to myself, huh?"

"You've tried, and you almost had me a couple times, but lying to yourself is a lot harder than lying to someone else."

Saint's cell phone rang. It was Olivia. He gripped it, telling himself that answering it would be a bad idea. He answered it anyway.

"Hello."

"I need to see you tomorrow at the salon."

"Olivia—"

"Please, Clayton, I really need to say something to you face to face."

"I don't know, Olivia."

"Please, Clayton."

He gritted his teeth.

"Are you there?"

"Yes, I'm here. I'll come by after work." Saint could feel her smiling. "I know you're smiling. What are you smiling at?"

"You remind me of a superhero. Math teacher by day and multi-lingual hustler by night."

"Goodnight, Olivia."

"Goodnight, Clayton."

Chapter 9

As Saint pulled into the Adult Learning Center's parking lot, his phone vibrated.

"What's up, Glenn?"

"I love you, man."

"I'm hanging up."

"I'm at Butta Cutz. Olivia told everybody the good news. The girls are planning on throwing you a party, but don't tell Olivia I told you. It's supposed to be a surprise."

"I'll try to act surprised."

"Saint…she's *really* feeling you. She's prancing around, telling everybody how you put the fear of God in Byron. She even gave Baby that raise she's been promising her for months."

"We don't have a future together, Glenn. So, don't take it there."

"You told her you were a math teacher."

"No, I didn't. She snatched my wallet and saw my ID before I could stop her."

"Bullshit! You're not that sloppy."

Saint smiled. "I got to go."

"Olivia said you were dropping by later on."

"Yeah, I'll be there after work."

"Jon-Jon finally showed his face. He told Olivia what you did to him, thinking she would be mad, and she told him if she was there, she would've told you to break both his arms."

"Talk to you later, Glenn."

Saint hung up and exited his car. As he headed up the stairs, the hairs on the back of his neck stood up like antennas. He had a layout of the center, the parking lot, and the surrounding area etched into his mind. The scenery had changed. An old, beige van with tinted windows was parked across the street. Without turning around to alert anyone who may be watching him, he headed inside and went straight to Principal Baker's office.

"Hi, Karen," he said to Baker's secretary. "Is he in?"

"Yes, he is."

"I really need to speak with him for a moment."

"Sure, one minute." She got on the phone. "Mr. Baker... yes, Mr. Andrews would like to speak with you..." She hung up. "Go right in."

Baker was seated behind his desk, going over some paperwork.

"Good morning, Mr. Andrews."

"Good morning, sir. I wanted to add a name to the students who will be taking the GED test."

Baker cleared his throat. "Uh, it's too late. The cutoff was last week."

Saint snapped his fingers. "Yes, you're right. Oh, well. Sorry to have bothered you."

Saint extended his hand. He purposely held his hand an inch out of reach. Baker shifted in his chair and reached for it. That's when Saint saw it. In an air-conditioned room, Baker's hand was wetter than the ocean's floor, and he had two gigantic sweat stains beneath his underarms. He had been talked to.

Saint turned to leave.

"Mr. Andrews."

"Yes."

"Your students...they've come a long way."

"Yes, they have."

"I had a talk with them earlier expressing my delight with them. I hope you don't mind, but I took the liberty of dismissing them for the day."

"Really?"

"Yes. It's summer vacation for Christ's sake. I figured a day off would show them that good grades are appreciated."

"That was very generous of you."

"It was the least I could do. As a matter of fact, why don't you take the day off? Your class isn't here, so you shouldn't be either."

"I really appreciate it. I'll see you tomorrow then."

Baker cleared his throat. "Yes, tomorrow."

Saint left the office. Karen saw him and put her fake smile back on.

"Everything okay?" she asked him.

"Couldn't be better," he replied.

If I ruled the world, CIA would stand for Clowns In Action, Saint thought as he headed to the boiler room. He stepped into the utility closet and removed the grid over the vent. Then he reached in and pulled out a duffel bag. He figured he had about fifteen minutes before the G-Men got antsy and sent someone into the center.

As he put on the dingy overalls, he re-enacted how the scene must've went down between Baker and the CIA. They probably walked in flashing their badges and started asking a thousand questions. Then they demanded to see the records of all male employees, especially the ones with impeccable backgrounds, because they knew all of his identities were airtight. Then they probably showed Baker obscured pictures they may have had of him, but none of them would look like Clayton Andrews. They allowed him to come into the center so Baker could identify him. Baker was probably wearing a wire, which explained why he cleared his throat so many times during their conversation.

He removed the thick moustache out of its case and used the pocket mirror to affix it to his face. Next, he took out a pair of contacts and put them in his eyes. He then fitted his afro wig and pulled a baseball cap low so the afro protruded out on each side. Afterwards, he stuck a piece of chewing tobacco in his mouth. His outfit was complete; it was time to Houdini.

"What's taking him so long?" Agent Ricks, the younger of the two agents posted in the van, asked.

"Be patient," his old-timer partner, Agent Dale, said. "He's probably using the can or getting something out of the vending machine."

"Or he's on to us and long gone."

"We have the center surrounded. We have men on the roof. We've even posted men on the adjacent roofs. The only way he's getting out of there without us knowing is if he flushes himself down the toilet," Agent Dale assured his partner.

"Do you think this is our guy?"

"Don't know, but someone high on the food chain seems to think so."

"Can you imagine the medals we're going to get if we put a collar on this guy?" Agent Ricks said, daydreaming.

"Medals? We'll be millionaires just off the interviews and book deals."

"I never thought of that."

"That's why I'm the senior agent," Agent Dale responded. He perked up. "All units, this is command. Someone's exiting the building. Standby." Dale looked over at Ricks, who was inspecting the suspect who had just exited the building. "Well?"

Ricks adjusted his binoculars. "Shit!" He scanned the clipboard that contained the roster of the center's employees. "Six-three, two hundred and fifty pounds, thick moustache, and a fucking afro. It's the janitor."

"Give me those." Dale took the binoculars from his partner and watched the janitor place a cardboard box by the dumpster before heading back in. "Shit! All units stand down. I repeat, stand down."

"We should send someone in."

"And risk being made? No, we wait."

Both men jerked to attention when the janitor came back out and placed two more boxes on top of the first one. He stood there for a moment and spit a glob of tobacco against the dumpster.

"What the fuck is he doing?" Ricks asked.

His question was answered when the janitor picked up the boxes and quickly carried them to his pickup truck.

"That thieving motherfucker. What the fuck can you steal out of a school?"

"Anything he could probably get his hands on to buy some crack," Dale answered.

They both watched the janitor get into his pickup and pull off.

"I can't believe we just watched him take off with all that stolen merchandise," Ricks said.

"I've been in this business a long time, Sonny Boy, and if there's one thing I've learned, it's this... Sometimes you got to let a lot of the small fish go in order to catch the big one."

Ricks was sopping up the jewel his seasoned partner shared with him, until the janitor who looked exactly like the one who pulled off in the pickup truck ran out of the center. He stood in the spot where the pickup had been parked, took off his hat, and threw it to the ground.

Ricks jumped out of the van, binoculars in one hand and his gun in the other.

"Somebody stole my truck!" the janitor told Ricks as he approached.

Agent Dale was already on the radio giving the description of the truck to the helicopters in the sky. Within minutes, they located the truck. All units converged on it. The only things they found in it were three cardboard boxes filled with shredded newspapers. Ricks was too young to know what was about to happen, but Dale had seen it too many times to count. For their blunder, he would be forced into retirement, and Ricks would be re-assigned to the file room located in the basement of some non-descript CIA building.

After reaching his getaway car, Saint pulled out his disposable phone and dialed Glenn's number. "Glenn—"

"Hi, Clayton," Grace said.

"Grace, put Glenn on the phone please."

"You sound agitated."

"It's an emergency."

"Is everything okay?"

"Grace, please, put Glenn on the phone."

"Okay, hold on." Grace handed Glenn the phone. "Your friend sounds like he has an attitude."

Glenn grabbed the phone. "What's happening?"

"Take care, my friend," Saint said, then hung up.

"Clayton! Saint!" Glenn pulled the phone from his ear and stared at it. A moment later, when his brain rebooted, he dropped the phone.

"Glenn, what's wrong?" Grace asked, a worried look coming over her.

Glenn's knees buckled and he crashed to the floor as he started to cry.

"Olivia!" Grace called out.

Everyone stared at Glenn and Grace as Olivia rushed toward them.

"Glenn, what's the matter, baby?" Grace asked, shaking him.

"He's gone," he said, hugging her.

"Gone where?"

Glenn got to his feet. "I have to go."

"Where are you going?" Olivia asked.

"I have to–" Glenn was shaking.

Grace grabbed him, but he broke free and ran out of the salon. He jumped in the middle of the street trying to hail a cab, but none was going to stop for a deranged-looking man.

Grace and Olivia ran outside and pulled him out of the street.

"Glenn, what's going on?" Grace asked, starting to cry.

"I have to get to his apartment."

"Olivia will drive you."

"No," he snapped. "I have to go alone. I have to stick to the plan. We planned... Oh God, I never thought..."

He darted out into the street in front of a taxi. It skidded to a halt. Glenn hopped in and shouted an address to him. The cabbie took off.

Glenn entered the apartment, rushing straight to the bedroom closet. He grabbed the 13"x18" aluminum attaché by the handle and carefully laid it in the middle of the floor. He sat cross-legged while fumbling for his keys. He pressed a five-digit code on the keypad attached to his key ring. If he hadn't and tried to open the case, a device inside would have triggered a small explosive that would have destroyed the documents contained within the case. He took a deep breath and opened it. The first document he came across was a statement for a bank account Saint had set up for him, with a balance of two hundred and fifty thousand dollars. The next document was a deed in Glenn's name to a house on 5th Avenue. The next item was a cell phone.

Glenn's heart rate went into overdrive when he heard the floorboard behind him creak. He reached for the last item in the case and rolled onto his stomach, with arms extended. He had Grace's head in the sights of the 9mm.

Grace's mouth formed a big O.

Olivia screamed, "Glenn, it's us!"

"How did you get here?"

"I saw Clayton's driver's license last night. I memorized his address."

"You shouldn't be here." He stood up. "We got to go."

"We're not going anywhere until you tell me what the fuck is going on," Grace said.

Glenn put the items back into the attaché and closed it.

"There might be some people on their way here. If we're here when they get here, they *will* kill us."

Grace and Olivia followed him out of the apartment, no more questions asked.

Glenn sat in the backseat of Olivia's car clutching the attaché case as they drove to his apartment in silence. When they walked through the front door, Glenn went straight to his room and slid the case into his closet. His eyes became heavy. His body was finally coming down from its adrenaline-induced high. He felt the heat rush to his face when he turned around and saw Grace staring at him from the doorway. He sat on the edge of his bed and took a deep breath. He ran his fingers through his hair as he exhaled. Olivia stood next to him with her arms folded.

"What's going on, Glenn?" Grace asked.

"I can't talk about it."

"You can't talk about it? You just had a gun pointed at me, Glenn."

"Grace, please, I can't–"

She took off the engagement ring, threw it at him, and walked off.

"Grace! Wait!" Glenn ran ahead of her and blocked the front door.

"I was about to be your wife," she said, starting to cry. "How can you just tell me that you can't talk about it?"

Glenn banged his head against the wall.

"Move!" Grace tried pushing him out the way.

"Wait!" He looked at Grace and then to Olivia. "Okay, let's go into the living room and have a seat. You got to be sitting down when you hear this."

Grace and Olivia sat on the loveseat. Glenn sat across from them trying to rub the goose bumps off his arms.

"God, where do I start?" he said out loud as he rubbed his arms faster.

"Start from the beginning," Olivia told him.

"The beginning. Okay…Saint's parents died in a car accident in France when he was two years old."

Grace cocked her head. "Saint?"

"That's Clayton's real name. At least that's the name I always knew him by."

"I remember Petrescu calling him that in Las Vegas," Olivia said.

"There was a young nun, twenty-three years old, who used to babysit Saint when his parents went to work. When they died, she brought him to the convent. The mother Superior left her in charge of taking care of him, and she raised him as if he were her own child. At the beginning of every summer, the young nun was sent to various convents throughout Europe, Africa, and Asia. She always took Saint with her."

That's how he learned all those languages, Olivia thought.

"One day, at the age of fourteen, Saint saw something he wasn't suppose to. In one of the nun's room, he heard a sharp scream. Being the curious boy he was, he went to check it out. He peeked through the keyhole in shock as the Father had the nun bent over a desk. Saint ran to the young nun, who he took to calling mommy, and told her what he had seen. She beat him and made him promise not to tell anyone. She made him understand that if the Father ever found out that he knew what was happening, he would send him away, and he would never see her again. He promised not to tell, but he also swore that if the Father ever tried anything with her, he would kill him."

Grace shook her head.

"About a month later, Saint heard arguing coming from the young nun's room. Saint stood a few doors away, recognizing the Father's voice. His heart did somersaults when he heard some scuffling and then a smack. He swore if the Father ever tried raping the woman who was his world, he would kill him, but saying it and doing it was two different things. It wasn't until he heard her choking that he bolted into action. He ran to the door and kicked it in. The Father had one hand wrapped around her neck, strangling the life out of her, while trying to put himself into her with the other. When the Father saw him, he backed up. Saint charged him and beat him mercilessly. The nun finally managed to pull Saint off of him. The Father was sprawled out on the concrete floor unconscious. Before he came to, the nun fled with Saint as far as she could.

Glenn stopped speaking for a moment before continuing.

"On their own, and with no one to turn to, Saint and the young nun did what they had to do to survive. Needless to say, the nun ditched the habit, along with her vows. She would find work as a maid, only to case out houses that Saint would break into and rob. He had worked his way into a small-time group of French thieves. They stole everything from clothes to cars. It was only a matter of time before he became recognized as their leader. With him calling the shots, the heists got more risky, yet more lucrative. He soon put the ex, young nun in charge of the clique."

"Josephine," Olivia whispered.

Glenn nodded. "Yes, the young nun. Saint went from being the leader to the enforcer. He made Josephine the most feared woman in France, and soon, there was not a continent she wasn't known on."

"So, the way you two met, was that a lie?" Grace asked.

"No, it was true. Only he wasn't working for Petrescu. It was the other way around. Petrescu was an accountant for the Rumanian mob, but he was working as a double agent for Josephine."

"Is he a teacher?" Olivia asked.

"Yes, he became a teacher after he…retired."

"Retired?" Grace looked at him suspiciously.

"Y'all are going to have to bear with me because the story gets kind of sketchy. From what I could drag out of Saint, Josephine started to believe he wanted to kill her, so she made a preemptive strike. She hired an assassin to kill him."

Both women listened in shock.

"And she would've killed him if it wasn't for me. I kind of had this bad habit of using Saint's spare key to get into his loft and just barge in."

"You sound like my brother," Olivia commented.

"That night, he brought *HER* to his loft, not knowing she was an assassin. Well, while they were doing their *thing*, she got on top and *whamp!* She stabbed him with a six-inch dagger right in the chest. As she yanked it out to slit his throat, that's when I busted in the door, not knowing what the hell I was walking into. The female continued her swing and let the knife fly right at me. The bitch caught me right here."

He pulled his collar down and showed them the stab wound high on his shoulder. Grace put her hands over her mouth.

"I brought Saint enough time for him to throw a right hook. The female rolled with the punch, landing feet first on the floor. He shot out the bed and grabbed his chest. Blood was pouring out of him like a waterfall. He fell to one knee and then fell backward against the wall."

"My God," Olivia whispered.

"When she saw him take what she thought was his last breath, she headed toward me to finish me off. Her face contorted into confusion when a projectile hit her in the back and flew out her chest. It took her a fraction of a second to realize Saint had shot her. She tucked her chin and did a roll to the bedroom door. She slid out the front door just as a bullet penetrated the wood where her head was a split second before."

"That's some crazy shit," Grace said, shaking her head.

"When Josephine found out her assassin failed, she begged Saint to forgive her."

"First, she wanted him dead, and then, she didn't?" Grace asked.

"No, I think she bought into the myth."

"The myth?" Olivia questioned.

Glenn took a deep breath, knowing what he was about to say would sound ridiculous to them. "Some believe Saint isn't human."

"Oh God," Grace said.

Glenn held his hands up. "People have sworn on the lives of their children that they killed him, but a few days later, these same people were... they disappeared."

Olivia stood up. "This is ludicrous. I can't believe I'm listening to this."

"Believe what you want, but Saint is the best at what he does."

"And what's that?" Olivia asked.

Glenn stood up. "You went to see Byron two days ago."

"Yes, and?"

"And Saint was there."

Olivia's eyes narrowed.

"After leaving Byron's office, you bumped into someone. Hazel eyes, dreads."

Olivia's eyes widened.

"Dr. Whitman," Glenn said.

"Impossible. That man looked nothing like Clayton. Height, build, nothing."

Glenn left the room and returned with a CD. He popped it into his stereo.

"Saint had a recording device embedded in his briefcase," he told them as he pressed Play.

"Dr. Whitman, please have a seat." Hearing Byron's voice made Olivia want to vomit. "Now, on the phone you were telling me of an invention of yours that will save lives."

"Yes, actually, it's a game and it can save your life." Olivia and Grace heard papers shuffling. "Here, take a look."

"This is when Saint hands him copies of his bank accounts and a warrant for his arrest," Glenn narrated.

"Wait, I don't understand," Olivia said.

Glenn held his hand up. "Just listen."

"This is impossible," Byron said, obviously staring at the copies of his bank statements. All three of his bank accounts, that held hundreds of thousand of dollars, now totaled a sum of three hundred and fifteen dollars. "An arrest warrant for forgery and fraud? This isn't true."

"The funny thing about the truth is it doesn't sell newspapers. They will have a field day with this. And even if you prove it was a computer glitch, your reputation will be long dead, and you'll only have three hundred and fifteen dollars to your name."

"I can't believe Olivia has this much power."

"Look beyond the owner, Mr. Turner. A lot of people stand to lose a substantial amount of money if you persist in your quest to try and destroy Butta Cutz."

"Unbelievable."

"All I'm going to need you to do is sign this document, and I'll be on my way."

Olivia remembered the contract she read with Byron's signature on it.

"Sure. Let me get my pen."

"This is where it gets good," Glenn said with a smile on his face.

Grace couldn't believe he was getting a kick out of the recording.

"Stay where you are!" Grace and Olivia heard Byron scream.

"Mr. Turner, put the gun down," Saint said, sounding irritated.

The women could hear Byron hitting something.

"The panic button you're hitting under your desk has been disabled," Saint told him.

"How do you know about that?"

"The same way I knew about that nickel-plated .25 you're pointing at me, which isn't loaded by the way."

"It *is* loaded."

"No, I took the bullets out myself."

"Bullshit."

"No, I distinctly remember taking the bullets out right after I broke into your safe that's hidden behind the bookshelf."

"What–"

"I didn't touch your coin collection, but the velvet bag filled with diamonds–"

Grace and Olivia could hear Byron shifting things and then opening what they assumed to be the safe Saint was referring to.

"Saint broke into his office the night before," Glenn informed them.

They could hear Byron cursing. "I need those diamonds back, my bank accounts restored, and this warrant dropped."

"And I need you to sign this document and have two of your employees witness it."

Use their own money to pay them. Olivia remembered what Saint said to her that night in Las Vegas.

Glenn stopped the recording.

"That didn't sound like Clayton," Grace said.

"It was him," Olivia said.

"How do you know?"

"I just know. Just like I know I will never see him again." Olivia looked at Glenn for confirmation.

He looked away. "It's better this way. Someone found him, and believe me, that's not easy to do. Whoever's after him will kill a dozen people just to get to him."

"So what is he going to do now?" Olivia asked.

Glenn shook his head. "Someone somewhere is going to be having nightmares for a very long time."

Chapter 10

It had been three weeks since Saint vanished, and Glenn carried around the phone he left behind like a security blanket. Every time he walked into Butta Cutz, Olivia would ask if he called. Soon, she didn't have to ask. She would just look at him, and he would subtly shake his head. On the outside, she seemed to be handling the situation well, but when she got home behind closed doors, she would break down. She couldn't understand how she could be so emotionally attached to a person who she barely knew. Right now, she should be angry with him for lying to her, leading her to believe he was someone he wasn't. But, she couldn't because she *did* know him. Whether he did it intentionally or unintentionally, Saint had revealed a piece of himself to her that night in Las Vegas and that day in her apartment.

It didn't matter if he was Clayton, Saint, or Dr. Whitman. It didn't matter if she was in his arms or if he was thousands of miles away. She felt connected to him, and she knew he felt the same way about her.

Love has reasons that Reason doesn't understand. She remembered him saying that to her in Las Vegas. She had asked him to say something to her in French, and of all the things he could've said, he said that. With the new information that Glenn shared about him, Olivia knew Saint was calculating. There was a reason for everything he did or said. What was he trying to tell her? That he loved her? He barely knew her. That's a question only he could answer, but he was gone. She knew she would never see him again, but that didn't stop her from whispering his name every night before drifting to sleep, praying he would somehow feel her calling out to him.

Grace tried to remove the blindfold when the cabbie told Glenn that they had arrived.

"Hold on," Glenn said, removing her hands from the blindfold.

"This is ridiculous. You know I hate surprises."

"You're going to love this one," he said, helping her out of the cab. When they stood in front of the co-op's entrance, he removed the blindfold and shouted, "Surprise!"

Grace stood there stunned as she stared at an elegant, Fifth Avenue home.

"Oh my God, Glenn."

"Let's go in."

Grace didn't move.

"What's wrong?"

"This place…it's so luxurious."

"You mean expensive?"

"We can't afford this."

"There's nothing to afford. It's already paid for."

"How?"

Glenn looked at her, raising an eyebrow.

"Clayton?"

"I found the contract in the attaché case. It was going to be his wedding gift to us."

Hearing the pain in his voice, she started tearing up.

"I told you, that's my boy." After a few moments, he grabbed her by the hand. "Let's go inside. I can't wait for you to see our home."

Grace stood in the lavished living room, staring out the huge picture windows. "The view is amazing," she gasped.

Glenn showed her the two master bedrooms, the gracious dining room, and the state-of-the-art gourmet kitchen.

"Our maid's name is Francine."

"We got a maid?"

"And access to the gym located on the first floor."

"I know Clayton paid for this, but are you sure we can afford to maintain this?"

Glenn held her hands and looked into her eyes. "Sweetheart, you know how we're taught that there are three classes of people: the lower, middle, and upper class?"

Grace nodded.

"Well, there's a forth. A class that the richest of the rich envy. A class whose wealth isn't money, and whose strength isn't power. People like Saint can have all the luxuries of the world given to them. All they have to do is ask."

"Sounds like a secret society to me," Grace mused.

"You have no idea. I spoke with the manager, and he told me the name of the man who owns this place. He's a French billionaire."

"Meaning?"

"A billionaire from France. Saint…France."

"Coincidence."

"No such thing when it comes to Saint."

Grace shook her head. "I can't get used to calling Clayton… Saint. Is he really that dangerous?"

"He's not dangerous at all. You just don't want to get on his bad side."

"Has this ever happened before? Him just up and disappearing?"

"No."

"And you're certain that he isn't coming back?"

"He once told me that he could never come back to a place where his identity had been compromised."

"And you're sure that none of us are in danger?"

"Positive. You saw me get rid of that gun."

"But there are people who know that you know him. People like Petrescu."

"Baby," Glenn said, caressing her face, "Petrescu is in that fourth class, and it took him decades to make it there. He's in heaven. The last thing he would want to do is come after Saint's only friend. He would be signing his own death certificate."

Grace sat on one of the oversized sofas. "All of this just seems so surreal. I was born and raised in the projects of South Bronx surrounded by rats, roaches, guns, drugs, and violence. The closest I ever came to seeing apartments like this was on the *Cosby Show*. And people like Saint, Josephine, Petrescu, and Marion Claude sound like characters out of a David Morrell novel."

"Sometimes fiction is nothing more than an author disguising the truth to protect himself from being sued or stepped to." Glenn knelt in front of her. "In three months, I'm going to be marrying a beautiful, *thick* Bronx girl. And by this time next year, my clothing line is going to be in every top-of-the-line clothing store. This is the happiest I've ever been in my life. I would've never gotten this far if it wasn't for Saint. He believed in me, he supported me, and he kicked me in the ass when I needed it. I only wish you and Olivia could've gotten to know that side of him."

Grace grabbed his hands and kissed them. "If he's half the man you've described him to be, I believe he will give us the chance to get to know that side."

As much as Glenn wanted to believe that, he knew Saint could very well be in Belem, a seaport in Brazil, selling catfish the size of Great Danes in one of its many fish markets. Not because he had to, but to learn the culture, language, and who's who in their underworld.

The Villa Kennedy in Frankfurt, Germany, is one of the most luxurious hotels in the world. There are 134 rooms and 30 suites. The ballroom can easily accommodate as many as 450 people. The spa includes a fifteen-meter indoor pool, a steam room, yoga and Pilates studio, a gym, and eight treatment rooms.

Ninety percent of the world couldn't afford to spend one night in the five-thousand-dollar a night suites. Nine-point-nine percent could, but did so sparingly. Then there was Josephine Delacroix, the point-one percent who was able to refer to one of its suites as home. Josephine had many suites in many different countries. Owning an estate on thirty-six acres of land with armed guards and a high-tech security system never appealed to her. To Josephine, estates and mansions were nothing more than clumsy shows of grandeur. In her lifestyle, clumsy meant certain death. No, she never liked the idea of being a sitting duck. Mobility and unpredictability saved her life on many occasions.

She rolled over on her queen-sized bed into the arms of her twenty-eight-year-old lover/personal bodyguard, Van. He wasn't Saint, but he was a quick study and obedient.

She slipped from between the silk sheets and headed for the bathroom. She stood in the shower, letting the hot water beat on her bronze-colored skin. Josephine looked to be no more than thirty-six, thirty-seven. She had her ballerina physique, dieting, and her personal trainer to thank for that. The only asset she attributed to her fifty-five years of age was her seasoned intuition. It was her seasoned intuition that caused her to put her men on high alert. After Saint contacted her and told her about his situation, she knew, just as he did, that only two people knew where he was. Claude and Petrescu would have to be taken care of.

Through the shower's opal glass, she watched the image of Van's blurry, naked body walk toward the shower. Without a word, he got in and stood behind her. He lathered up a sponge and began washing her back. He slowly worked the sponge to the front of her body while inching up on her from behind.

"I love you," he whispered in her ear.

Josephine felt his manhood throbbing against the small of her back.

"I love you," he said repeatedly, as he lathered her breasts the way Saint used to.

"Get out!" she barked without warning.

Van tried nibbling on her ear, but Josephine pulled away from him and turned to face him. Her steel-gray eyes dug into him like claws. Van rinsed off and stormed out. Josephine finished washing up and then returned to the bedroom.

"Get dressed. I'm hungry."

Van didn't move from the couch.

"Did you hear what I said?"

When he didn't answer, she stepped around the couch and stood in front of him. "What's your problem?"

He stood up calmly. "You know what my problem is."

"I'm not going through this with you. Either you get dressed or I'll find someone to take your place."

Josephine walked off, but Van ran in front of her, stopping her progress.

"What do I have to do to get him out of your heart and me into it?"

Josephine caressed his cheek and spoke to him in French.

"Saint is not in my heart; he *is* my heart."

Van pulled his face away from her touch. Josephine grabbed him by the back of the neck.

"Remember your place," she hissed.

Her gray eyes seemed to turn dead black as her grip tightened on the back of his neck. He swallowed his pain and bowed his head.

"Get dressed," she said, walking away from him. "We're going to Silk's."

Silk, the highly-renowned restaurant, was on the east end of town. There were restaurants much closer, but Josephine didn't want close. She wanted Silk.

Josephine's three-car convoy arrived. Van watched as a man from the front car and one from the rear car got out and gave the surroundings a quick look over. Both men nodded subtly to let him know the area was clear. Van exited the driver's side of the middle vehicle and walked to the back to let Josephine out.

She took his hand and exited the heavily-modified S-class sedan. The maitre d' met them at the entrance with a smile that could block out the sun.

"Good to see you again, Miss Delacroix. We've been expecting you."

Josephine stopped in her tracks and looked at Van.

"I called ahead to make sure we had a table," he said, shrugging his shoulders.

"You idiot. Get me out of here."

"What?" Van asked, looking alarmed.

Josephine spun to rush back to the car. Her quick turn saved her life. Instead of the sniper's bullet piercing her back and ripping through her heart, it hit her high, dislocating her right shoulder. Van knocked her to the ground while the armed guards exited their cars and drew their guns, searching for a target.

CLACK!

A split second later, one of the guard's head snapped back, spraying blood straight into the air.

CLACK!

Another guard's head snapped to the left. As the rest of the guards shot in the general direction of the sniper's gunfire, Van hit the keypad on his key ring, opening the rear door of Josephine's car. He dragged her unconscious body into it and slammed the door shut behind them. He heard the screeching of tires. Two SUVs careened around the corner, heading for them. Van hopped over the front seats. The sedan roared to life and he peeled off. The gunmen in the SUVs hung out the windows shooting.

The Brabus 6.1 UTV, or Urban Tactical Vehicle, was a heavily-modified S-Class. One car of many that Saint had out-fitted for Josephine. Van remained cool as he heard the clinking of bullets hitting the car. He knew the UTV was lined with lightweight Kevlar padding. And the windows were shatterproof, blast-proof, and could withstand multiple rounds at close range.

Van dipped in between cars, nearly sideswiping one. The jostling caused Josephine to become semi-conscious.

"Saint?" she whispered. "Saint, what happened?"

Van gritted his teeth at the sound of his name. He took a chance and looked in the back to check her condition. The front of her shirt was blood soaked. He lifted the armrest and flipped the second red switch. A signal would be sent to Josephine's team of backup bodyguards who were on standby at the Villa Kennedy. They would track their GPS signal and meet up with them. He just prayed he could make it to the safe house before Josephine lost too much blood.

Josephine cried out. "Saint! My shoulder, it hurts."

"Try to relax," Van cried out. "I'm going to take care of you."

Josephine didn't respond.

Van's grip on the steering wheel tightened as it jerked to the right. One of the gunmen's bullets had shot out one of the front tires. The tires were run-flats, so Van was able to quickly regain control of the Mercedes. He was coming up on a hairpin turn. He took a deep breath and flipped the fourth red switch. Just below the rear bumper were dispensers to release the tank full of oil slick contained in the trunk. He growled as he hit the hairpin turn at nearly fifty miles an hour. He barely made it. The two SUVs weren't so lucky. As soon as they yanked their steering wheels to the right, the SUVs spun out of control. Van heard a loud crash and then an explosion.

Two black UTVs identical to the one he was driving were heading right for him. The backup had come. He zoomed past them and looked in the rearview mirror. They spun around and caught up with him. One drove in front of him while the other one positioned itself behind him. Van grabbed the walkie-talkie off the console.

"Pull over," he said.

At the shoulder of the road, Van hopped into the backseat to check Josephine's injuries. One of the armed guards approached the car.

"Get in and drive to the safe house!" Van ordered.

The man hopped in, told the other two cars their destination, and then pulled off. Van ripped Josephine's blouse open. The bullet had gone through clean. He sighed. He used her shirt to cover the wound and then laid her head on his lap. Josephine winced. He could see that her shoulder was dislocated.

"We're almost there," Van told her.

He saw her lips moving, but he couldn't make out what she was saying. He leaned his head down as close to her lips as he could.

"Saint," she whispered, "kill 'em alllll."

At a monastery near the Dambulla caves located in Sri Lanka, India, a taut-bodied monk poured buckets of water over his body. The water matted his curly afro to his head. His scraggly beard made him look much older and less dangerous than he really was. The kids giggled as the cold water cascaded down his body, causing him to shiver. They scattered as he spun around and threatened to throw what was left in the bucket at them.

He used his hands to wipe the excess water off his body, then unwrapped his orange robe from around his waist and put it on.

Today, the monk planned on walking the countryside, begging for food and engaging in heavy meditation. The character of the soul-searching monk was one that Saint found to be most fulfilling. He loved simplicity. He got more of a fulfillment from begging for food and helping others than living a life of loftiness. Living high, he believed, made a person arrogant, lazy, and weak. He loved the trenches. They kept him rooted and sharp. But, most of all, the trenches allowed him to keep an ear to the ground and his finger on the pulse of people.

No matter how far away he distanced himself from Olivia, he still couldn't stop thinking about her. That's why he traveled all the way to India. He knew for a fact that if he remained anywhere in the Western hemisphere, he would go back to New York, and that was a chance he knew even the Saint couldn't risk.

There were only two people who knew he was in New York: Marion Claude and Petrescu. He thought back to a couple nights ago when he had Petrescu dangling off of his penthouse balcony by his ankles. As bad as he wanted to release him and watch him bounce off of the street below, he knew he was telling the truth. He didn't give him up. He didn't go after Marion Claude yet. He wanted Petrescu to call him and tell him what was going on. He wanted Marion to stew in the juices of paranoia and flinch at every sudden gust of wind for a while.

As he grabbed his begging bowl and started to head out of the monastery, an old monk called out to him. Saint bowed to him and walked over. The old monk led him out of the monastery and to his dwelling down the road. He pointed to the satellite phone and said something in his Hindi language. Saint made out a couple of the words. The phone started ringing, and he had rushed to get him.

"Don't worry," Saint said, struggling with the Hindi language. "It will buzz again." He didn't know the word for ring.

The old monk smiled and then bowed.

Saint and the monk had an interesting history. Josephine had introduced them seven years ago. A broker from Korea convinced the monk's niece that a wealthy Japanese businessman was interested in marrying her. The businessman came to Sri Lanka and they were married, but he had to rush back to Korea for an important meeting. He left the monk's niece a plane ticket and promised to meet her at the airport when she arrived two weeks later. When she arrived, the broker met her at the airport and told her that he would first take her to where she would be working and then to her husband.

Unbeknown to the naïve girl, the broker dropped her off at a brothel. Six months later, the girl was able to smuggle out a message to her uncle, who turned to Josephine for help. That's where Saint came in. Five days later, the brothel mysteriously burned down with its owners still inside. Saint returned to Sri Lanka with the monk's niece, and the monk was forever indebted to him.

The old monk smiled when the phone rang again.

Only one person had this number. Saint answered it.

"What's up?"

"Saint."

Her voice was so low that he had to put his hand over his other ear to hear.

"Josephine?"

"Saint, I need you."

"What's wrong?" He could hear the phone being taken from her.

"Saint, Josephine was shot."

"Who is this?"

"My name's Van."

"What happened?"

"We were on our way into a restaurant—"

"Which restaurant?"

"Silk."

"In Germany?"

"Yes. Josephine had a funny feeling and she turned to go back to the car. That's when it happened."

"That's when what happened? Be specific."

"A sniper shot her high in the shoulder."

Saint dropped his head. The monk could see the pain in his expression and gave him some privacy.

"How could you let this happen?" Saint growled.

"Hey—"

"You're her personal bodyguard, right?"

"How do you know that?"

"If you weren't, she wouldn't allow you to be on the phone with me right now."

"Yes, I'm her personal bodyguard," Van said with authority.

"Then it should've been you who took that bullet, not Josephine."

"Wait a minute."

"Where are you now?"

Van didn't respond.

"Don't fuck with me!"

"We're at the safe house in Frankfurt. Hello? Hello?"

Saint turned disconnected the call and sat on the dirt floor. He rubbed his temples. A soothing thought sprinted through his mind. He looked around the simple hut and imagined him and Olivia sitting on the ground of a hut of their own, eating red rice and okra. That calmed him down. He took a deep breath. Someone had given him up to the CIA. Now, they had made an attempt on Josephine's life.

As he sprung to his feet, he could feel the thrill of the hunt coursing through his veins. He bowed to the old monk and explained to him that he had to go. The monk went into his bedroom and retrieved Saint's duffel bag.

"Thank you for your hospitality." Saint grabbed his bag and left.

Chapter 11

The safe house was a dental office. The receptionist eyed the man who just walked in wearing a pair of slacks and a sweater.

"Can I help you, sir?"

"Yes, Dr. Randal is expecting me."

The receptionist eyed his scraggly beard and dreads, which hung freely about his face and shoulders.

"Name?" she said, looking at her clipboard.

"Jordan...Michael Jordan."

The receptionist looked up, visibly shaken.

"Yes," she said, fumbling with some folders on her desk before standing up. "Please follow me."

She led Saint past the offices, down the hall, and up a staircase. At the top of the stairs, he spotted one of Josephine's men. He pulled out the orange handkerchief and wrapped it around his left hand, identifying who he was. The man immediately nodded and allowed him entry, but he stopped the receptionist.

Saint walked down the long corridor toward the room with four sentries posted in front of it. The wall of men parted for him to enter.

Josephine was lying in bed with a bed tray in front of her. The young man, who was trying to get her to eat something, spun around when he heard the door open.

"Saint," Josephine called out weakly, but her smile was strong. She held her good arm up for him to come to her.

It was Van's first time seeing the infamous Saint. *He isn't all that,* he thought, sizing him up. He stood up from the edge of the bed and walked toward him.

"I'm Van. We spoke on the phone," he said, extending his hand.

Saint cut his eyes down at the hand and then walked past without a word.

Van's face contorted with anger. He made a fist with the rejected hand and closed his eyes. *He is NOT all that.*

Saint bent down and allowed Josephine to put her arm around his neck and kiss him on the cheek.

"You know I hate facial hair," she said, tugging at his beard.

"It's my new look." He examined her. "Looks like you've lost a lot of weight."

"I've been trying to get her to eat, but she—" Van stopped in mid-sentence when Saint threw him a look over his shoulder.

Saint sat on the edge of the bed and looked at the tray of food. Sirloin steak, mashed potatoes, and string beans. He picked up the fork and knife, cut a piece of the steak, and put it in his mouth.

"Pretty good."

"I'm not hungry," Josephine said.

Saint cut another piece of the steak. This time, he held it to her lips.

"I said I'm not hungry."

Saint made a tsking sound with his tongue. "Open!"

Reluctantly, she opened her mouth and bit down on the steak. Van was furious. It took Saint two seconds to do what he'd been trying to do for two days. He shook his head as Saint fed her some mashed potatoes, string beans, and some more steak. He wanted to stab him with the fork when he saw the way Josephine stared into his eyes as he wiped her mouth with a napkin.

"Wait outside," Saint said, without turning around to face Van.

When he didn't move, Josephine fixed him with a stare that gripped his heart. He sucked his teeth and exited the room.

"Of all the men you have, you got this kid as your personal bodyguard?"

"Don't start with me. Not now." She touched his face. "I missed you."

He gently grabbed her hand and removed it from his face.

"You have any idea who did this?"

"Marion Claude. Who else?"

"What makes you so certain?"

"I know it was him. Don't ask me how. I just do."

Saint shook his head. "This wasn't part of our agreement."

She squeezed his hand. "I almost died, Saint."

He got quiet.

She pulled his hand to her lips and kissed it. "I miss the convent. Leaving it has plagued my soul all these years."

"I kind of miss it myself."

"You know what I miss most about it?"

"What's that?"

"I miss *our* innocence. We were each other's world. Nothing else mattered to us." Saint moved to stand up, but her grip tightened on his hand. "Sometimes it takes tragedy to stop us in our tracks and take a closer look at our lives."

"Don't tell me a bullet to the shoulder has helped you develop a conscience."

"I'm done, my love."

"Done with what?"

"With all this. When we were living on the streets and begging for scraps, I thought if we were to ever strike it rich, all of our problems would disappear. The funny thing is, they did. We were no longer homeless; we were no longer hungry. But, those problems disappeared only to make room for a new set of problems. All the sins I've committed; all the enemies I've created. My most painful regret is that amidst my sinning and transgressions, I lost sight of what mattered to me the most. I've lost the only person in the world who has ever meant anything to me. I am not a bad person, my love." Josephine began to cry.

Saint kissed her on the forehead. "No, you're not a bad person."

"I still can't believe I tried to have you killed," she said, turning her head.

Saint turned her head back to face him. "That was pretty fucked up, huh?"

His dark sense of humor brought a smile to her face.

"I have a favor to ask of you, my love. I swear by God that it will be the last thing I will ever ask you to do for me."

Saint looked away.

"I can never go back to being a nun, but I want to go back to a simple life. As long as Marion Claude is alive, I can never do that."

"You must be heavily drugged, Josephine. Go back to a simple life? It's too late for that."

"It's never too late."

"We've made our beds, and we have to lie in them."

"No," her voice cracked. "Don't ever believe this is it for us. We've done some terrible, terrible things, but we don't have to continue like this. We *can* change. We *can* be forgiven."

For the first time since they left the covenant, Saint was staring into the eyes of Josephine, the nun, who he used to turn to for guidance and love.

"I take care of Marion and then what?"

"That's it. I disappear. I'm out of your life forever."

"Josephine, I want to believe you so bad, but I can't see you cooking your own meals and washing your own clothes."

"I welcome the day when I can do those things again. I may not look it, but I'm an old lady. It's time for me to retire while I still can. Will you do this last thing for me?"

Saint stood up and gazed into her eyes. "I'll call you when it's done."

"Daaayum! My shit is tiiight! This is the shit right here," Fire, an up and coming rapper, said as he stared at his haircut in the mirror. "Niggas told me that you was the bomb, but, man, you is the *bomb*, Olivia. That's my word. I'ma shout you out on my next song. As a matter of fact, I need a barber for when I go on tour and—"

"Whoa, slow down now. I appreciate the business and the compliments, but I don't travel."

"Yo, there's plenty of money in it. Plus, you get to meet all kinds of celebrities."

"She don't need to meet no celebrities. She is a celebrity," Grace said.

"No doubt. I'm from Tennessee, and your name is ringing bells way down there. That's why I had to come see if the hype was true."

"Is it?" Baby interjected.

"No doubt. This place is everything niggas said it was and then some."

"Fire, I know you don't mean any harm by it, but I would appreciate it if you wouldn't us the 'N' word in here," Olivia said.

"Oh, my bad. I didn't know you took offense to it."

"You should take offense to it, as well."

"It's just a word."

"What if a white boy walked up to you and said, 'Hey, Fire. What's up, my nigga?'"

"Nah, see that's different."

"Different? It's just a word."

"Yeah, but when a white person says it, he don't mean it the way we mean it."

"You don't know how *any* person means it when they use it. Don't assume just because a black person uses it that he's using it with the best intentions."

"True story. Not only can I get my haircut by the hottest and prettiest barber in the country, but you dropping jewels, too? I'm feeling your energy right now," the nineteen-year-old said, staring at her like he wanted to eat her alive.

Olivia snapped him out of his trance when she brushed the hair off of him and unclipped the barber's cloth from around his neck. He hopped out of the chair and dramatically reached into his pocket and pulled out a chunk of money. Baby, Grace, and Olivia cut their eyes at each other. Fire was rocking six platinum chains; each had a saucer-sized, iced-out showpiece weighing it down. On the front of his platinum teeth, he had FIRE in red diamonds. Olivia was about to drop another *jewel* on him about his *costume*, but she knew he wasn't ready for that one just yet. He peeled off two one-hundred-dollar bills and handed it to her.

"This is way too much," Olivia told him.

"For having the pleasure of being in your presence for two hours, it's not nearly enough."

Olivia wasn't going to take the young rapper's money, but the stare Baby and Grace shot her changed her mind.

"The next time you're in New York stop by, and the next cut is on me."

"Next time I'ma bring some of my crew along."

As Fire walked out the front door, Olivia exhaled.

"That's it. I'm done," she said, sitting in her barber chair and leaning back. "Miki, flip the sign to Closed."

"Already ahead of you," she said, walking back from the door.

Olivia slipped off her shoes and let her hair down.

"What's on the agenda for tonight?" Grace asked everyone.

"Sleep," Baby said. "Right after my ex-boyfriend breaks me off a little sumthin' sumthin', and I kick his ass out."

"Correct me if I'm wrong, but ex-boyfriend means he used to be your boyfriend and now he's not," Olivia said.

"You're right. He used to be my boyfriend. Now he's my fuck buddy. And when he can't satisfy me anymore, he'll be my ex-fuck buddy."

"Play on, playa," Miki said. "I'm going to the Lotus," she said, dancing in her chair.

"Damn, girl, you stay up in them clubs," Baby commented.

"That's where the action's at. And you know me. I loves me some action."

"I didn't see you doing that much action when we were pounding Lynise and her hoe-ass friends out," Baby said.

"Girl, you bugging. You saw me with that bat in my hand, ready to bust somebody's melon to the white meat."

"You damn near busted yours open when you swung at Lynise and missed. If that bat was made of rubber, it would've wrapped around your neck and choked you to death," Grace said.

Baby and Olivia started cracking up.

"All right, ladies," Olivia said. "Baby is going to get her booty call. Miki, the club head, is going to the club. And we all know Grace is going home to cuddle up with her boo. So, y'all go on and get out of here. I'll close up tonight."

"Why don't you come to the club with me?" Miki asked.

"Yeah," Baby agreed. "You really should go."

"I'm too exhausted. I'm not twenty-five like you, Miki. So, after a hard day's work, I just want to crawl into bed."

"Girl, age ain't got nothing to do with it," Miki said. "All you got to do is chug down two Red Bulls, and you'll be good to go."

"Shit, all she got to do is chug down one of them cups of coffee I make for her every morning, and she'll be good to go," Baby said.

"Go! Get the hell out of here before I change my mind and leave y'all here to close up."

Baby and Miki picked up their things with the quickness.

"You don't have to tell me twice," Baby said.

"See y'all tomorrow," Miki said. Both women broke out.

"And what do you think you're doing?" Olivia asked Grace, watching her grab the bucket of cleaning supplies.

"What does it look like I'm doing?"

"Put that down and get out of here."

"Don't worry. Glenn isn't going to miss me. He's too busy preparing for that fashion show next week."

Olivia got out of her chair and walked over to Grace.

"I got it. This is my quiet time."

Grace looked at her. "You got to move on. He's not coming back."

Olivia smiled. "It's not even about him anymore. I just want to find what you and Glenn have."

"And you will. You just have to give someone a chance."

"I will, when the right man comes along."

Grace shrugged her shoulders. "I'm going to call you when I get home."

"I'll talk to you then."

Olivia walked her to the door and locked it behind her. Then she went to her office, where she took off her shoes and slid her feet into a pair of slippers. She headed to the espresso machine and poured herself a cup. That's when she heard keys jingling in the front door.

"What did you forget this time, Grace?" she asked without bothering to turn around.

"I forgot how beautiful you look."

Olivia spun around and almost spilled the coffee on herself. "Oh my...God."

Saint took in her beauty. Olivia was wearing a pair of Daisy Duke shorts and a sleeveless halter-top. His eyes ran along her curves and tones.

Olivia's first reaction was to scream when she saw the shaggy hobo standing in the middle of her salon. Saint had lost weight, and his appearance was...scary.

"What happened to you?"

"It's a long story."

"Why am I not surprised? How did you get a key to my shop?"

"It's a long–"

"Please don't say it. You're starting to sound like a broken record. What are you doing here? I thought you never come back to a place where your identity has been compromised."

"Glenn could never keep a secret."

"Don't blame him. It was only right that he tell me everything about you."

"He didn't tell you everything about me."

"Yes, he did. He told me all about the convent and Josephine..."

"So he *did* tell you everything."

"That's what I said. You still didn't answer my question. What are you doing here? And don't tell me it's a long story."

Olivia followed him to the back, where he sat in her barber chair.

"You owe me a haircut."

"You're joking, right?"

"Do I look like I'm joking?" he asked, pointing to his matted hair.

"I can't do this. It's eight o'clock, I'm tired, and I just remembered that I'm mad at you."

"Mad at me? For what?"

"For what? How about you lied to me from day one. You said you were an accountant."

"I said I worked with numbers."

"You said your name was Clayton Andrews."

"It was."

"You didn't tell me who you really are."

"That's not considered lying."

"Oh God, I hate you," she said, balling up her fists.

"I *love* you."

Olivia blinked. "You need to leave."

Saint got out of the chair and approached her. She put her hands up in front of her, stopping him from coming any closer.

"You just need to go."

"Don't ask me why or how, but I do love you. And I came all the way back to New York, risking the death penalty or life in prison, just to tell you face to face."

Olivia avoided looking him in the eyes.

"Yes, I...lied to you. I misled you. My whole damn life has been built on lies and deception, and I thought there was no changing that. I just accepted my life for what it was. However, someone made me realize there's hope for me. I've thought about a life other than this one, but I never believed it was possible. If I had a choice to be anyone in the world, you know who I would be?"

"Who?"

"An honest man."

Olivia squinted her eyes at him.

"I want to be honest with you. Please give me the chance."

"Sit in the chair."

"What?"

"I said sit in the chair. You came for a haircut, right?"

Saint looked over his shoulder at the chair and then back at her. He took a few steps backward until his heel touched the chair and then sat in it. He watched Olivia as she closed the blinds and turned out all the lights except the ones at her station. She walked back to him and spun the chair so he could face the mirror.

"Take a good look. When I'm done, you won't recognize your own self."

Olivia turned the chair back around so he couldn't see the mirror. She grabbed a pair of shears and walked around him, contemplating what she was going to do with his hair.

"Aren't you supposed to put some kind of apron or smock on me or something?"

"Are you telling me how to do my job?"

"No, I'm just saying—"

"How 'bout you don't say anything, and let me do what I do?"

She kicked off her slippers, slowly climbed onto the chair, and straddled him. Saint opened his mouth to say something, but she rested the shears on it.

"Not a word." She grabbed the afro pick hanging off her chair and gently picked his hair. "Your hair is clean."

"Of course it is."

She dropped the pick and grabbed a handful of his hair. "So, Mr. Honesty, what's your real name?"

"Honestly?"

"Please."

"Saint…Christopher."

"Wow, Saint Christopher. Do you have a last name, Saint Christopher?"

"I'm kinda new at this telling-the-truth thing, so some things I'm going to have to learn how to divulge."

"Like your last name?"

"Yeah, like my last name."

"Umm, I see." She ran her fingers through his hair and started to snip away at the excess hair resting above her fingers.

Saint had trouble keeping his cool. Between Olivia sitting on his lap and her cleavage in his face, it became difficult for him to breathe.

"Is it me or is it hot in here?" he asked.

"It's you…and me. Am I making you uncomfortable?"

"Honestly?"

"Please."

"Yes."

"Good," she said, snipping at a couple more strands of hair. "Hold these for me."

She handed him the shears, while reaching for the spray bottle on her shelf. Arching her back to do so brought her pelvis right down on his hardening shaft. She smiled at him devilishly when she felt him throbbing under her. He gasped when she sprayed the cold water on his head. She grabbed the towel off of the armrest and brushed the hair off his face.

"I'll take those back now," she said, referring to the shears.

She grabbed them from him and gave him the spray bottle to hold. For the next twenty minutes, she snipped away without a word. Every now and then, she would arch her back so the softness of her crotch could meet the hardness of his.

"Sit still," she said, smacking his hands off her waist.

"You're torturing me."

"No, I'm giving you a haircut."

Aiming the spray bottle, he squirted himself in the face a couple times. Olivia smiled.

"Don't even think about it," she said, reading his mind.

"What?" He sprayed her.

She snatched the bottle from him and threw it. They locked eyes. Saint then dropped his eyes to the front of her wet shirt and saw Olivia's nipples shooting out against the fabric. She grabbed him by the hair, pulled his head back, and gazed into his reddish-brown eyes.

"Your eyes were dark brown when we met."

"Contacts."

"And these are your real eyes?"

"Yes."

She inspected them and gently kissed his right eyelid, then his left. He started to grab her by the waist. She tugged on his hair.

"Don't touch me. I haven't forgiven you yet."

"I'm about to explode."

"You do and I'll cut it off," she threatened, snipping at the air with her shears.

Olivia grabbed the towel and wiped the excess hair off his head and face again. She ran her hands through his freshly-cut, curly hair, while at the same time leaning his head back. She stared at his lips before gently grazing them with hers. Next, she ran her tongue across his top lip and then the bottom one. Sitting up, she looked at his teeth.

"I know for a fact that gap between your front teeth wasn't there before."

"I was wearing false fronts."

She shook her head. "You are unbelievable. And your cheek bones are more pronounced."

"I'm not wearing mouth implants. They used to make my face seem a little more–"

"Rounder?"

"Yes."

She kissed each cheek as she played with his beard. "Is this real?"

"Yes."

"What about the mustache?"

"Yes."

"What about this?" she asked, grabbing his penis.

"Hell yeaaah."

"You said you were going to be honest."

"Oh, I'm Honest Abe right now."

"It's kind of hard for me to believe you, seeing how the round-faced, dark-eyed, no-gap-in-the-front-teeth man I used to know was a fake."

"There's nothing fake about that," Saint replied, looking down at his crouch.

She climbed off of him. "Let me see it."

"Stop playing."

"Do I look like I'm playing?" she asked, putting her hands on her hips.

"You serious?" he asked, looking around.

"What are you looking around for? There's no one here."

"What if someone walks by the shop?"

"The blinds are closed. No one can see inside."

"Can't we go to your office?"

"Show it to me right here, right now, or I don't want to see it at all."

Saint's leg started to shake. "You're enjoying this, aren't you?"

"I'm waiting," she said, tapping her foot.

He unfastened his pants and pulled them down.

"Drop those, too."

He groped at the waistband of his underwear and pulled them down.

Olivia sized him up and nodded. "Okay, I believe you."

She unsnapped her shorts and stepped out of them. Then she unfastened her top and dropped it next to her shorts.

"Lace underwear. Nice."

She climbed back on top of him. He inhaled sharply when she dabbed the tip of his penis with her juices.

"And their crotchless."

Before he could get his next words out, she covered his mouth with hers. He grabbed her by the waist, and this time, she didn't stop him. As he started to push himself inside of her, she jumped.

"Shit!" She hopped off of him and ran to Baby's workstation, tearing it up during her search.

"What are you doing?"

"I know Baby has a box of condoms in here somewhere. I just saw them the other day."

"Olivia."

"I think I found them. Shit, this ain't them."

"Olivia."

"Hold on."

"Olivia," Saint said more sternly.

She turned around, panting. When she looked down at his soldier, he was wearing a helmet.

"You brought some with you?"

"Yes."

She walked back to the chair, eyeing him suspiciously. "You planned this?"

"Honestly?"

"So help you God."

"I didn't know what to expect, so to be on the safe side—"

"The safe side?"

"Safe side, safe sex. You know."

"All I know is you disappeared out of my life, and now you just waltz back in it and are sitting in my chair naked from the waist down with a condom on."

"You're right. This doesn't seem right."

He hopped out of the chair, but Olivia shoved him back down and climbed on top of him.

"Every time I'm on the verge of forgiving you, you do something to upset me." She positioned herself and allowed him to penetrate her. "I should be cursing you out right now," she moaned, "but it's been so long."

She bit down on his shoulder when he buried himself inside of her.

"How long has it been?" he whispered.

She made a guttural sound and threw her head back as her body convulsed and released.

"Too long."

She rode him to another orgasm, and then another, and then another. Saint prided himself on being able to control his ejaculation, but when Olivia unclasped her bra from the front and stuck her dark brown nipple in his mouth, he bit down on it and exploded inside her.

"That's it?" Olivia asked, curling her upper lip.

Saint climbed down from the barber chair with her legs still wrapped around him. "Don't move."

He reached into the crook of the chair where he had stuffed the box of condoms and pulled one out. With his right hand, he brought it up to his mouth and ripped the packet open with his teeth. At the same time, with his left hand, he removed the used one off his penis. With the dexterity of a magician, he worked the condom out with his right hand and rolled it onto his still rock-solid shaft.

"Cocked and ready to rock."

He walked with her wrapped around him to her office and laid her across her desk. He tossed the used condom in her wastebasket and then threw her legs on his shoulders. Olivia held onto the edge of her desk as he hammered into her like a piston. She growled as her body spasmed out another orgasm.

Saint pulled out and flipped her over like a rag doll. With her feet planted firmly on the floor, he bent her over the desk and entered her from behind. Olivia matched his thrusts until he came for a second time.

"Time out," she said, barely able to make a T with her hands. Saint pulled out of her and exited the office.

"Where are you going?" she called out to him.

"I left the box of condoms on the chair. Be right back."

Olivia's eyebrows shot up.

Olivia's eyes popped open when she heard Grace scream her name.

"What the hell, girl? I was worried half to death about you. I called your house and didn't get an answer. Then I called your cell. When you didn't pick up, I called here. Why didn't you answer the phone?"

"Wha...where..." Olivia was lying under a blanket on the couch in her office. She shot up, remembering the all-night romp session all over the salon.

"Nah, ah," Grace said, covering her eyes. "Where your clothes at, girl?"

Olivia looked down and realized she was naked. Her clothes were folded neatly on the mini bar. She wrapped herself in the blanket and ran out into the salon. The place was spic and span clean.

Baby and Miki looked at her like she'd just escaped from a mental institution.

"You okay, ma?" Baby asked.

"Yeah," Olivia croaked and then cleared her throat.

She rustled her hair as she looked around the salon. She knew last night wasn't a dream. Every muscle in her body ached. She tottered back toward her office.

"What…in the world happened to you? If I didn't know you the way I do, I would think you got with a man last night," Grace said.

"Baby!" Olivia tried to shout, but her voice cracked.

"What's up?"

"Coffee…please. Extra caffeine, extra large."

"I got some on right now," Baby responded, casting her a sidelong glance.

Grace followed Olivia into her office. "Are you okay?"

"Can I have some privacy?" Olivia's voice was totally hoarse now.

She shooed Grace out of the office and rubbed her eyes. Grace's words echoed in her head. *If I didn't know you the way I do, I would think you got with a man last night.*

Shit, Olivia thought. No man she ever came across could do what Saint did to her the whole night. She looked on her desk to see if he had the courtesy to at least leave a note. There was none. She dropped the blanket and got dressed.

"Grace, I'm going home."

"I just fixed your coffee," Baby said, holding the tall brew of mud.

"I'll be back later."

Olivia was exhausted and becoming angry. Saint had walked back into her life and walked back out just as quick. She hadn't planned on having sex with him, but when he disappeared, she regretted not having sex with him. All she could think of last night when she saw him was she might not see him again. She had to be with him, even if it was only one time. But now that her pent-up frustration had cum down, she was thinking clearly. The last thing she should've done was sleep with him. Not only did he take her to new heights, she could already feel her body starting to crave more of him.

When she pulled up to her house, she felt moistness between her legs. *Shit,* she thought. *Just thinking of him got me all messed up.*

She opened her front door and heard music playing from the kitchen.

"Jon-Jon, is that you?" She took off her shoes and headed toward the kitchen. "I told you about just barging up in here and helping yourself to all the food in my refrigerator."

She stopped in the doorway when she saw that the man cooking in her kitchen wasn't Jon-Jon.

"What took you so long to get here?" Saint asked, flipping the last omelet onto a plate.

Olivia just stared at him.

"What?"

"You know what. How do I wake up on my couch with no recollection of how I got there or how the salon got straightened up?"

"The four glasses of wine you had last night during our freak fest probably had something to do with it."

Now that he mentioned it, she remembered pouring wine in his belly button and slurping it up.

"After I straightened up, I came back into the office and you were snoring."

"I snore?"

"And mumble. Anyway, we agreed I would get a head start and meet you because we couldn't risk the chance of anyone knowing I was back."

"I don't remember that."

Saint dropped the spatula. "You didn't tell anyone I was here, did you?"

"No, I didn't. I told the girls that I was going home to get some sleep and would be back later."

He walked from around the counter with two plates of eggs and hash browns and placed them on the table.

"You look good in an apron."

"Last night you said I looked good with nothing on."

"You *definitely* look better with nothing on," Olivia said, sitting down. She dug into the food without waiting for Saint to return with the glasses of orange juice.

"You worked up an appetite, huh?"

"I usually don't eat like this," she said in between wolfing down the eggs and gulping the glass of orange juice. "My body is shaking. I feel like I haven't eaten in days."

"Hmm."

"Not to mention these eggs and hash browns are banging."

"Hmm."

"Is that coffee I smell brewing?"

Saint got up and walked to the stove. "Freshly brewed. Heavy on the caffeine, light on the water, right?"

"You read minds, too?"

"That's what some people believe."

"What am I thinking right now?"

"You're thinking…a hot bath would feel good right about now."

"That's not what I was thinking, but now that you mention it, it does sound like a good idea."

"Maybe drop about six oil beads in there, a little lavender bath salt to soften the water…"

"Yes, that'll work."

"Maybe light a scented candle."

"I'm feeling that."

"And the icing on the cake is me sitting behind you massaging your shoulders and neck, 'cause I know you're aching."

"And how do you know I'm aching?"

"Stand up."

Olivia started to stand and winced.

"That's how I know." He brought her cup of coffee to her. "Sip on that, and I'll go get your bath ready."

Olivia took a couple sips of her coffee and gagged. It was just the way she liked it.

Five minutes later, Saint came back downstairs. "Almost done."

He smiled when he walked into the kitchen and found Olivia had put her head down and dozed off at the kitchen table. He walked up behind her and kissed her on the neck.

"I'm up," she said, jerking awake.

He pulled the chair out and scooped her up in his arms. Then he walked with her to her bedroom and laid her on the bed.

"Just give me a few minutes."

Saint smiled and started undressing her. He pulled her covers over her and caressed her cheek.

"I have something to tell you."

"What is it?" she asked.

"I have to disappear for a while."

Olivia sat up. "What are you talking about?"

"In order for me to be with you, I have to do this one last thing."

"Does this one last thing include killing someone?"

"Honestly?"

"Please."

"Maybe."

She became silent.

"I'm going to do everything in my power to try and resolve this without anyone having to die. Usually, I can do that."

"And what if you can't this time?"

He didn't respond.

"I can't let you do this. If you have to kill someone to be with me…then maybe it's not meant for us to be together."

"This person is a piece of shit."

"But he is still a person."

"I thought you wanted to be with me."

"God knows I do." She gripped his hand. "But not if you have to murder someone."

She felt a chill run down her spine as she watched the whites of Saint's eyes turn coal red.

"This is crazy," he said, standing up. "I must be losing my mind."

"Wait," Olivia said, getting out of the bed and grabbing his arm. She jerked her hand away. The arm she grabbed a hold of felt nothing like the one she held last night. The muscles in his arm felt like steel coils poised to strike.

"I can't change who I am. I can never have a normal life. I got half of the world's law enforcement after me and the entire underworld murdering anyone who they think is the Saint."

"Listen to me for a second—"

"There's nothing to listen to," he said as he stormed toward the bedroom door.

"Saint Christopher, please."

He turned around and slowly walked back toward her like a panther about to pounce on its prey. Olivia backed up until her back was against the wall. His lips were inches away from her ear.

"Never mention that name…again," he growled.

Too stunned to move, Saint was out the front door and out of her life before Olivia felt safe enough to peel herself off the wall. She experienced firsthand why so many feared him. The Saint wasn't a man who became a beast when provoked. He was a beast, period.

Chapter 12

"You know you could've stayed home and got some rest, right?" Grace said to Olivia.

"No, she couldn't," Mr. Ryan butted in. "Olivia always cuts my hair on Saturday afternoons."

"One Saturday wouldn't have killed you, old man," Grace retorted.

"If I would've walked in here and Olivia wouldn't have been here—"

"Calm down, old man," Olivia said. "Sit still before I accidentally zeek you."

"You ain't never zeek nobody, so if you zeek me, it would be on purpose."

"Actually, she did zeek somebody," Baby said. "Remember that politician running for governor a few years back?"

"That wasn't by accident," Olivia admitted. "He was a creep. Remember him, Grace?"

"Yeah, the one who was on TV talking about how his wife is the backbone to his success, and then the following week, he's sitting in your chair trying to be your sugar daddy."

"She already gots a sugar daddy," Mr. Ryan said.

"That's right, sugar daddy," Olivia said, kissing him on the cheek. "Can I have five hundred dollars, sugar daddy?"

"Shiiit, I ain't even got enough to pay for this fifty-dollar haircut. I remember back in my day when a man could get a cut, a shave, and a hell of a conversation for a quarter."

"This ain't the fifties, pop," the teen sitting in Grace's chair said. "Prices rise, pop. It's called inflation."

"Call me pops again, and the left side of your face is gonna be inflated."

Everyone, including the teen, started laughing.

"You got that, pops...I mean, boss playa."

"Damn right. Recognize a playa when you see one. I was a playa when the game was *The Game*, when the playas played by the rules, when honor and respect weren't just words. They was your life."

"Honor and respect still exists," the teen said. "Only they're known by different names. Heckler and Koch."

Mr. Ryan shook his head like he just sucked on a lemon.

"Damn ghetto cowboys. I remember when Huey Newton used guns to fight for our rights."

"Huey who?" the teen asked.

"Huey who?" Mr. Ryan repeated in shock. "Huey Newton, one of the founders of the Black Panthers."

"I heard of the Black Panthers, but I never heard of that cat."

"What? Who was the other founder?" Mr. Ryan asked Olivia.

"Bobby Seale."

"What year was it started?" he asked Grace.

"In the sixties, I believe."

"Nineteen sixty-six," Miki said.

Everyone turned in her direction.

"What? I remembered that from high school."

Mr. Ryan looked at Baby. "Who was their minister of information?"

"History ain't my thing, Mr. Ryan."

"Anyone? Who was their minister of information? With all these black folks up in here, somebody's got to know."

Everyone looked at Miki.

"Don't look at me," Miki told them.

"Eldridge Clever," a woman said, standing by the front door. "He also wrote a series of essays that were later collected in his book *Soul On Ice*, which was published after his release from prison."

The shop grew silent. The woman admired the salon's deco and nodded when she recognized some of the paintings on the wall. She wore a black and gold pants ensemble, and the patchwork Kimono jacket was open to reveal a matching bustier top. Her black satin pants ended at the back of her Luichiny stilettos. Her hair was fashioned into a soft-layered cut with frosty highlights. It was curled and styled to frame her face. Her teardrop diamond earrings and diamond necklace mesmerized anyone who stared at them too long.

Olivia looked down at the woman's right wrist and couldn't help but admire the different colored diamond bracelets. Some were white, some canary yellow, and others pink. There were ten in all. Her makeup was flawless.

When she locked eyes with Olivia, she walked toward her. Her walk would tell anyone that she was important, royalty even. Back straight, chin up, shoulders squared.

"I've never seen you around here before," Mr. Ryan said, remembering how to talk.

"That's because I'm not from around here," she said, not taking her eyes off of Olivia's.

Olivia didn't hear it before, but she heard it now. The woman spoke with a slight accent.

"Miss Martin." The woman extended her hand.

Olivia shook it. The woman's hand was deceptively rough and surprisingly strong.

The teen stared her up and down. "How did you know the answer to that old-ass question, ma?"

"I'm not as young as I look."

"And I'm not as old as I look," Mr. Ryan said, winking.

"Forgive me," Olivia said, "but I can't place your face right now. Did we ever meet?"

"Not formally, but we know of one another through a mutual friend. My name's Josephine Delacroix, and I've been dying to meet you."

Olivia's heart dropped to her stomach.

Josephine was the only one who picked up on Olivia's initial shock. The thing that everyone else did pick up on was the fact that neither woman had released the other's hand.

"If it's not too much trouble, is there someplace we can talk?" Josephine asked.

"Ah...sure." Olivia put her clippers down and washed her hands.

"Hey, hey, you didn't finish cutting my hair," Mr. Ryan said.

"Grace will finish you off."

"You know that nobody touches my head but you."

"Well, then, sit here until I get back."

"What the hell—"

Olivia was escorting Josephine to her office before Mr. Ryan could finish his sentence and before everyone else could figure out what just happened.

When Olivia closed the door behind them, it seemed like the room temperature dropped a few degrees. She rubbed the goose bumps on her arms as she sat behind her desk.

"Have a seat."

Josephine refused to sit. "If I don't sit behind the desk or at the head of the table, I don't sit."

"Well then, can I get you something to drink?"

Olivia started to stand, but Josephine stopped her.

"I'm fine." She looked around the office. "Is this where you spent the night with my Saint?"

"Excuse me?"

"Saint walked in here eight o'clock last night and he didn't leave until six this morning."

Olivia stood. "I think you better leave."

"I think you better lose that attitude before I forget that I'm a lady."

"Are you threatening me?"

Josephine kicked off her stilettos and walked up to her. Even with her heels off, Olivia still had to look up to her.

"Don't let that phony kickboxing class you're taking get your ass kicked up in here."

Olivia's eyes widened.

"I know everything about you and all four of your brothers." Josephine grinned when Olivia's stance softened. "I just want to talk."

"Then talk."

Josephine backed up. "I don't know how much you know about Clayton."

"You mean Saint Christopher?" Olivia couldn't wipe the smug smile off her face when she saw the shocked expression on Josephine's.

"How much do you know about him?"

"He's lied to me so much that I don't know what's true and what's not."

"That's my Saint."

Olivia exhaled. Initially, she was going to tell her everything Saint shared with her just to prove Saint had shared things with her that he never shared with anyone else. At the last moment, she realized if she revealed that she knew too much, Josephine would have a bullet put in her brain.

"I didn't come here to threaten you or cause any bad blood between us. Saint and I have a long history together. One that is stronger than blood and more precious than life. Right now, he has to do what many would call a suicide mission. In order for him to do what he has to do and survive, he can't be distracted in any way."

Olivia shook her head.

"I need Saint *Christopher* to be the Saint. If he isn't at a hundred percent, he *will* die, and that would kill me. And I refuse to be the only one losing someone dear to me. Now, what I want is simple. If you care for him at all, you will end whatever it is you think you two may have."

Josephine's subtle threat bit into Olivia's soul.

"What if I love him?"

"Sometimes our love is tested by letting go of that which we love most. If you *really* love him, you will let him go."

"Even if I wanted to let go, I have no way of contacting him."

"I know my Saint. He will see you tonight before he leaves." Josephine slipped her shoes back on and smiled at her. "I trust you will do the right thing."

Olivia folded her arms and looked away.

Josephine walked to the door and opened it. "A little word of advice. Your receptionist, Miki, met a tall, light-skinned man at the club last night, and she agreed to have dinner at his place tonight. Tell her to cancel. He's raped every woman he's ever been with."

"And how do you know this?"

"He works for me." Josephine exited the office.

A few minutes later, Olivia walked back to the floor.

"You okay?" Baby asked.

"Miki, you're going out with a tall, light-skinned man for dinner tonight?"

"How'd you know that?"

"Call him and cancel."

"Why?"

Olivia walked up to her and whispered in her ear what Josephine shared with her. Miki picked up the phone. She couldn't dial dude's number fast enough.

"Hey," Mr. Ryan called out to Olivia as she headed toward the front door.

"Not now," Olivia said, without looking back.

Josephine controlled her breathing as she got to within ten feet of her car. Van climbed out the backseat and ran to her. Josephine collapsed in his arms.

"You should've never come here. Your wound isn't fully healed," he hissed. "I could've taken care of this myself."

Josephine shushed him as he helped her into the backseat.

"Take us to the hotel," he told their driver.

Josephine reached for the handkerchief in his shirt pocket and dabbed her forehead with it.

"I had to come," she said weakly. "I had to see her for myself. Had to let her see me, make her feel my words."

Van opened a bottle of water and put it to her lips. She took a couple sips.

"Are you one hundred percent sure Saint didn't see you tailing him?"

"I'm a hundred and ten percent sure."

Josephine stared at him.

"If he knew I was following him, would he have led me here last night or to her house this morning?"

"I'm too close. I can't afford any mistakes."

"I don't make mistakes."

"Neither does he."

"You should've let me take him out when I had the chance."

Josephine put her finger to his lips. "I can't let anything happen to you. When this is over, you will be my new Saint."

Van beamed with pride.

Josephine laid her head back on the headrest and stared out the window. No matter how many men she'd been with, she only loved Saint. She didn't care where she was or who she was with, whenever he called, she was there. That was their understanding.

When she hired the female assassin to go after him, it wasn't to kill him. She only wanted to test his love for her.

"Seduce him," she remembered telling her. "Do what you have to do to make him fall in love with you."

"And then what?" the assassin asked.

Josephine didn't answer her then and there because she knew her Saint. She knew he would pass the test. He could never love another.

"I've been seeing someone," she remembered him telling her one night. "She's incredible. She might be the one."

"The one? What are you talking about?" Josephine asked him.

"I think I may be falling for her."

It was five years ago, but the pain she felt in her heart now just thinking about it was just as sharp as it was five years ago.

"Do you love her?"

"I think I'm starting to."

"But you love me?"

"Yes, but our love is different."

It took every fiber of her being to maintain her composure that night. As soon as he left her villa, she called the assassin, and in a blind rage, she gave her the order to kill him. She wanted her to stab him through the heart.

"Josephine, are you okay?" Van asked.

"Yes, I'm fine."

She had poured her heart out to Saint in the dentist office. She wanted to leave her life of stress and just disappear. The only thing she didn't tell him that day in the safe house was when he killed Marion Claude, she wanted the both of them to disappear and live a simple life together the way they did at the covenant.

When Van called her at the hotel last night and told her that he followed Saint to the salon and he didn't emerge until the crack of dawn, she knew Saint loved Olivia. And when she looked into Olivia's eyes, she knew she loved him, as well. He betrayed her once again. This time, him living would not be an option.

When Olivia left the salon, she went straight to the precinct to see her brother. Josephine had put the fear of God in her. Saint, Josephine, Marion Claude, Petrescu, she finally realized just how dangerous they were. Mike had offered to have a cop car posted outside of her house, but she refused. She just wanted to put him on point. They agreed that they should all get together at the salon tomorrow afternoon and figure out what the next move should be.

Now, she lay wide awake in her bed . Josephine said Saint was leaving that night and would be by to see her. She loved him, but as much as it hurt her to admit, she could never be with him. They could never have a normal life together. Saint would forever have to look over his shoulder.

She jumped when the phone rang. She looked at the caller ID. When she didn't recognize the number, she got butterflies in her stomach. She let it ring six times before answering.

"Hello."

"Before you hang up, give me a chance to apologize for the way I came at you this morning."

Hearing his voice gave her goose bumps.

"Are you there?"

"Yes, I'm here."

"Is everything okay?"

"No."

"I should be doing this face to face. I'm coming over."

"Where are you?"

The doorbell rang.

"At your front door."

Olivia sprung out of bed and reached for the pair of jeans she threw on her chair earlier. She then put on one of her oversized sweaters and pulled her hair back into a ponytail.

When she opened the front door, she barely recognized the man standing in front of her. Saint was dressed in all black. He was wearing an unzipped, three-quarter lambskin jacket. Under it, he had on a double-zip merino sweater and a pair of wool, pinstriped slacks. His loafers were calfskin, and his glasses were a pair of gold-filled titanium with onyx flecks. He dyed his hair and beard, giving them a salt-and-pepper look.

"Can I come in?"

His eyes were dark brown, his face rounder, and the gap between his front teeth was gone.

She moved to the side to let him in. "You're leaving tonight, I see," she said, eyeing the leather weekend bag he was holding.

"Yes."

"Nice disguise. You look like a middle-aged corporate executive going on a business trip. If we were on the same plane sitting next to each other, I wouldn't even recognize you."

"Sure you would. No matter how hard we try, we can never fool those who are closest to us."

Olivia turned her head.

He placed his bag on the floor and took a step toward her. "You asked me about the scar on my chest last night."

"And you refused to talk about it."

She knew the story from Glenn, but she wanted to hear it from him.

"There was a woman... before *Her*, I was only with one woman."

"Josephine."

"Yes. I should've known Josephine was testing me. She always tested people's loyalty to her, especially mine. The way Candice and I met, I just knew there was no way Josephine could've been setting me up."

"How did you meet?"

"At a café in France. One I'd never been to before. I just walked in to grab a cup of coffee. She was a waitress. At least that's what I thought at the time. I did a thorough background check on her and everything checked out. But, of course, it would. Josephine never did anything half-ass. To make a long story short, I fell in love with her. When I told Josephine that I was thinking of retiring from our criminal lifestyle and settling down, she hugged me and told me that she was proud of the man I'd become." Saint closed his eyes as he tried to swallow the pain swelling in his throat. "She even helped me pick out the ring."

"A ring?"

"I was going to ask Candice to marry me."

Olivia was blown away. Glenn didn't share that piece of information.

"A few nights later, at my flat, I proposed to her and she accepted. We celebrated, we…made love, and the moment I let my guard down, in that fraction of a second, Candice drove a knife into my chest."

Saint's voice had changed to a deadly whisper as tears of rage came to his eyes. Olivia reached out to touch him. She pulled her hand away when he shrank back from her.

"I vowed to never love anyone like that again." He said something in French. A phrase Olivia remembered from Las Vegas.

"Love has reasons that Reason doesn't understand," she said.

He smiled. "You have a good memory."

She made another attempt to touch him. This time, he didn't move. She caressed his face and stepped into his arms.

"You smell like an old man."

"I thought women liked Brute."

"Yeah, old women."

They both smiled.

"I love you, too," she said, reading his mind.

"When this is over, I will come back to you. I promise."

"No," Olivia said, with tears forming in her eyes. "You can't come back."

"But you said you love me."

"And I do. God knows I do. But, love isn't going to protect us from your enemies."

"I'll protect us."

"You know that's impossible. The only reason why you've survived this long is because you're a ghost. The moment you become human, they will be able to catch you or worst. Your enemies will use your love for me to draw you out."

He looked away as a tear ran down his cheek.

"You know what I'm saying is true."

"I can find a way for us to be together."

Olivia shook her head. "I love you, Saint Christopher, and I would give anything to spend the rest of my life with you, but we both know that's not going to happen."

She started crying.

"Loving you and knowing that I can't be with you is killing me. I don't know how much more pain my heart can take. Please, if you love me, just leave and don't come back."

"Olivia—"

She turned her back on him.

He picked his bag up and wiped the tears from his face. When he got to the front door, he stopped.

"MacKalister," he said without looking back.

Olivia looked over her shoulder. "What?"

"Last night you wanted to know my last name. It's MacKalister."

As soon as Olivia turned around, he was out the front door. When she got to the front door, he was gone. She ran down the steps and looked up and down the street. Like the ghost he was, Saint had vanished.

Chapter 13

Twelve hours on one plane and then five hours on another gave Saint nothing but time to think. Think about Olivia. There had to be a way for them to be together. Nothing was impossible. He just needed time to figure it out.

La Gomera, a part of the Canary Islands a few hundred miles off the coast of Africa, was where he exited the interisland seaplane. He had arrived at La Gomera's port, San Sebastian, just before midday. He hadn't been out of the plane's air-conditioned cockpit a full ten minutes before sweat trickled down his chest, back, and underarms, staining his cotton T-shirt. Even with shades on, he had to squint against the sun's glare. A few moments later, he walked into a yellow and green shack surrounded by banana plants.

"Can I help you?" the pleasantly plump woman behind the desk asked.

He recognized her voice from their phone conversation.

"Yes, I called and reserved a car two days ago," he said without bothering to remove his shades.

"Name?"

"George Wilham."

She typed the name into her terminal. Saint could tell from her bone structure and accent that she was from Spain. She flashed him a courteous smile as she waited for his name to appear on her screen.

"Ah, yes, Mr. Wilham. I see you right here. Mid-size, correct?"

"Yes."

"I just need to see your identification and have you sign right here," she said, pulling out a pre-printed rental agreement.

"And I'll take one of these," Saint said, picking a map from the rack and tucking it in his back pocket.

"You're all set." She slid back his license and credit card to him, both in the name of George Wilham, and a set of car keys. "The red Plymouth parked behind the jeep," she said, looking over his shoulder.

"Thank you."

After hopping into the rental, he unfolded the map on his lap. His eyes landed on the intersection he had to get to. He shot through the narrow streets like a thread through the eye of a needle. Behind his calm demeanor, his eyes and ears were attuned to everything, from the faces of every person he passed to the tropical storm watch warning issuing from the car's stereo.

Forty-five minutes later, he arrived at the intersection. He eyed the bar where he was supposed to meet his contact at fifteen minutes ago and hoped the man hadn't got spooked and left.

Walking in, Saint headed toward the cigarette machine. His eyes found the thin man sitting at the bar the moment he entered the establishment, but he didn't want to step straight to him without drawing a quick schematic sketch of the weather-worn building and its patrons. When he first walked in, the thin man spotted him immediately, but dismissed him. And why wouldn't he? Saint's appearance had changed drastically from the night they first met. The thin man was Marion Claude's chauffeur.

That day in front of Butta Cutz, when Marion Claude was getting into his limo, Saint stole a glance at the chauffeur and caught the split second look of hatred the thin man shot at Marion Claude. Without Saint realizing it, his instincts surmised that the chauffeur was the weak link in Marion's armor.

With all the glamour and glitz revolving around Marion Claude, no one ever paid attention to the chauffeur. Of all the men Marion employed, his chauffeur worked the hardest and was the most under appreciated. He was on call 24/7, a gofer, baggage handler, the butt of every joke, and often times a whipping boy when Marion needed to take his frustration out on someone.

A chauffeur knows his employer better than anyone else. He knows his favorite foods, wines, and women. There are even times when he overhears snippets of conversations taking place in the back of the limo that would be worth thousands of dollars to the right person. To a person like Saint.

After Marion Claude's razzle-dazzle display at Butta Cutz, his driver dropped him at the Bryant Park Hotel for the night. Saint followed the disgruntled employee to a bar on the lower East Side and made him a deal he couldn't refuse. Every chauffeur's dream. Appreciation, praise, and a lot of money.

Saint asked one of the patrons sitting at a table, nursing a glass of Jack Daniels, where the bathroom was. The man pointed a shaky finger. Saint thanked him and headed for it. From what he could see, there was only one exit: the front door. There were no other rooms aside from the bathrooms and a door that looked like it led to a storage area. None of the men or women in the bar looked threatening. He headed toward the bar and made eye contact with the bartender.

"A shot of vodka," he said, sitting next to the chauffeur.

The thin man looked at the heavyset, salt-and-pepper haired gentleman and nodded.

Saint cleared his throat and greeted the man in French. "Good to see you again, Vince."

Vince recognized the voice and downed the rest of the vodka in his shot glass before looking at Saint. "I'm sorry. I didn't recognize you," he responded in French.

"That was kinda the point, Vince."

"I thought maybe you changed your mind and weren't coming."

"The trip was longer than I expected."

Vince looked at his watch. "I'm cutting it kind of close. I have to hurry and get back."

"So talk quick."

"He's been here ever since you did something to Petrescu. Hanging him off a balcony or something. Since then, he's been trying to contact Josephine, but she's not taking his calls." Vince leaned in closer to Saint and whispered, "He's talking crazy."

Of course he is, Saint thought. *He's been a prisoner in his estate for the past month. A man who's not used to being in the same place more than a few days at a time tends to get a little jittery and erratic.*

"The estate is impregnable. He never leaves; he doesn't even walk in front of the windows. He has an army of men on twenty-four hour watch, most with automatic weapons and guard dogs. He even has men testing the food and water for any chemical agents you may have slipped into them. He's impossible to get to. I don't see how you're going to—"

Saint cut him off with a look. "You better head on back. The money will be deposited in your account tomorrow morning."

"Don't you want to know which bedroom he's staying in this evening? He stays in a different one every night."

"You were only obligated to tell me where Marion Claude disappeared to if he decided to run, and you have."

"For the amount of money you're paying me, I thought you would want me to do much more."

Saint patted him on the shoulder as he stood to leave. "There is one more thing I need you to do."

Vince winced as he mentally kicked himself in the behind for pressing the issue.

Saint leaned down and whispered in his ear, "Tell Marion I'm here and that I'm going to kill him."

Saint navigated the dizzying roads out of San Sebastian onto a road that led him through fields of banana plants and palm trees whipping dangerously in the wind. Over the radio he heard the radio announcing a tropical storm advisory being issued for the umpteenth time. A cover of blackness blanketed the sky, and before he had a chance to look up, raindrops the size of quarters pelted his windshield. He pulled over and got out. He closed his eyes as the warm rain bounced off his face. A gust of wind, almost strong enough to whisk him off his feet, slammed him against his car. He quickly climbed back into the safety of his car. He knew if he couldn't get into Marion's compound, he would just have to get into his mind. Telling Vince to warn Marion that he was there was the first step of his plan. Next, he had to get his hands on some weapons.

"Start from the beginning!" Marion Claude shouted.

Spittle flew out of his mouth and onto the face of Vince, who didn't dare wipe it off.

"Boss, I've already told you five times—"

"And you will tell me five thousand more times if I choose to hear it again. Now start from the beginning."

"I walked into the bar in San Sebastian and ordered a drink. A few moments later, a man sits besides me and says, 'Tell Marion I'm here and I'm going to kill him.' Then he got up and walked out."

"He tells you that he's going to kill me and you just let him walk out of the bar?"

"Boss, I…I…I…my head…so many things were going through it. At first, I could do nothing but sit there in shock. Then I ran to the payphone and called you."

Marion struck the man standing next to him on his chest.

"Get on the phone. I want more men flown here immediately."

"Sir, we already have twenty well-trained men."

"I want twenty more! Do as I say. NOW!"

"Yes, sir."

"And you," Marion said, sticking his pudgy finger in Vince's face. "You do know that he will kill everybody here, including you, just to get to me."

"I wasn't thinking—"

"Which is why you will never be anything other than a driver. Get out of my sight before I have you cut up into small pieces and fed to the dogs." Marion screamed for his assistant. "Jean!"

"Yes, Marion." She popped her head in from the other room.

"That bitch is still avoiding my calls?" he asked, referring to Josephine.

"Yes, sir."

"Any word from Jimmy?"

"Last I heard from him, he and his men had landed in Germany and were heading to Josephine's suite at the Villa Kennedy, but I don't think she's there, sir."

"I don't pay you to think. I pay you to do what I say without question."

"Yes, sir."

"Keep calling her until she answers." Marion jumped as the lights flickered off and on. "What the fuck!"

"It's the storm, sir," Jean told him.

Marion shook his head. "Get what's his name on the phone. The one who was with Saint in Las Vegas."

"Glenn Lemora, sir?"

"Yes. Get him on the phone now!"

In New York City, at the Apollo Theatre, Glenn was sitting backstage rubbing his temples and taking deep breaths.

"There you are," Grace said, walking up on him. "I've been looking all over for you." She hugged him and could feel him trembling. "Boo, stop worrying. Everything is going to be just fine."

"It should be. I've spent the last two weeks, day and night, ensuring that everything tonight will be perfect."

"And it's going to be."

"This is it, baby. Tonight, we are officially unveiling Beauty-full clothing to the public."

"Mr. Seeger is really coming through for you. He got your fashion show at the Apollo, like he promised; he's introduced me to at least five potential investors already; and…Puffy can't wait to meet you."

"What? You saw him?"

"Mr. Seeger introduced me to him."

Glenn started wringing his hands.

"C'mon, boo," Grace said, rubbing his back. "Talk to me. What's really bothering you?"

"It's just that…I've never done a show without Saint. He had a way of making me believe in myself. Whenever I got nervous, I would just look for him in the crowd and he would give me that look."

"And what look was that?"

"That I'm-gonna-kick-your-ass-if-you-embarrass-me look."

"Did it look like this?" Grace stared at him through the slits of her eyelids as she tightened her lips against her teeth.

"Yeah, that's it."

"Well, Olivia and I are going to be in the front row. So, if your self-esteem needs some boosting, just glance our way. Trust me, we'll be giving you that look."

Glenn straightened out his three-piece, double-breasted electric blue suit and kissed her lightly on the lips. "That's why I love you so much."

"After the show, I have a surprise for you."

"Really?"

"I picked up a little something from Victoria's Secret this afternoon."

"A little something?"

"A *little* something."

Glenn bit his bottom lip and looked her up and down.

"Focus on the show. You'll have the rest of the night to focus on me."

"I love you."

"I know you do," Grace said, while seductively walking off.

Glenn was feeling himself so much that he put a little more man into his voice when he answered his cell phone. "Talk to me, but make it quick."

"Mr. Lemora, my name is Jean. I'm Marion Claude's personal assistant. Please hold."

Glenn's hand started to shake as he fought to keep the shakiness out of his voice. "I don't have time to—"

"Glenn! We have a serious problem."

"I don't know what you mean."

"I mean you better contact Saint and call him off."

"Call him off? Mr. Claude, I haven't seen him or heard from him since—"

"Let me put it a different way. I don't care how you do it, but you contact him and you make him understand that if anything happens to me, you won't be paying for a wedding. You'll be paying for your fiancée's funeral."

"What—"

"I have men in the theatre right now. All I need to do is give the word. Am I making myself clear?"

"Marion, wait—"

Glenn's last words were spoken to a dial tone. Shaking like a leaf, he tried dialing Josephine's number. He cut his phone off and shut his eyes so tight that he started seeing tiny red dots. He calmed himself and steadied his fingers as he tried dialing her number again. It rang about thirty times before someone answered.

"May I help you?"

"I need to speak with Josephine right away."

"Miss Delacroix isn't available at the moment. May I take a message?"

"Make her available! I need to speak with her immediately!"

"Sir, if you would like to leave a message—"

"Saint told me to call."

The voice on the other end didn't respond.

"My name's Glenn Lemora. I have a message for her from him. It is important that she gets this message right now!"

"Please hold." The forty seconds Glenn was on hold felt like forty years. "I'm connecting you now, sir."

Glenn tapped his foot as the phone rang.

"Yes."

"Josephine, Marion Claude just called me."

"And?"

"And he's going to kill my fiancée if I don't call Saint off. What the hell is going on, Josephine?"

"Nothing that concerns you."

"What? Did you hear what I just said? He's going to kill my fiancée."

"Don't worry about him. He has more important things to worry about than sending someone to kill your precious fiancée."

"He doesn't have to send anyone. They're already here in the theatre."

"Really?"

"Call Saint off, Josephine. Please."

"I'm sorry, Glenn."

"Josephine, please don't do this."

"Goodbye, Glenn."

Glenn kept begging on his phone long after Josephine hung up.

"Glenn, are you okay?" Mr. Seeger asked as he walked up on him.

"I have to get Grace out of here." He tried to push past him, but the fifty-year-old caught him off guard when he slammed him against the wall. "You listen to me very carefully. You have a show to do and you're going to do it. You try to get Grace out of here, and Marion's men will kill her."

Glenn's complexion paled.

"Marion called me as soon as he hung up with you. He wants you to call off Saint."

"I can't."

"And we don't want you to."

"We?"

"My men will be sitting right behind Grace and Olivia. I give you my word, nothing will happen to them. By the end of the show, Marion Claude will be dead, and you will have nothing to worry about."

Seeger backed away from him as one of the models headed toward them.

"Glenn, I can't get this latch to stay fastened," she said, turning her back to him to take a look at it.

"Stay focused," Seeger said, then flashed him a crooked smile and walked off.

Glenn pushed the model out of his way and threw up in the wastebasket.

Van knocked on Josephine's suite five minutes after she called for him. She opened the door and let him in. She was wearing a nightgown and her hair was pinned-up.

"Were you asleep?" she asked.

"I won't sleep until we're out of this grimy city," Van spat.

"New York City isn't so bad."

"It's terrible. When are we leaving?"

"Soon. I just got a call from Glenn Lemora."

"And?"

"He's having a show at the Apollo tonight."

"You already knew that."

"What I didn't know was Marion Claude called him threatening to kill his fiancée if I didn't call off Saint."

"Figures he would do something like that."

"And he has men in the theatre."

"He probably does."

"Do we have anyone there?"

"Why?"

"Do we?"

"No. I didn't see any reason to send anyone. Should I now?"

"No." Josephine walked to the door. "Goodnight."

Van walked to the door, and acting as if it was an afterthought, he asked, "You want me to stay?"

"If I wanted you to stay, I wouldn't be standing at the door saying goodnight." She watched the vein on his forehead appear and then throb.

Van nodded and left.

Saint continued driving on the main road. The rain had stopped momentarily and the sun was just ducking below the horizon. When he looked up in the rearview mirror and saw the flashing lights, a smile appeared on his face. He had been looking for the police. Instead, they found him. He would just have to improvise. He pulled over to the shoulder of the road and rolled down his window.

The officer climbed out of his yellow SUV and walked up to Saint's window. "Sir, it's pretty nasty out here. You should be indoors. This storm is going to get worse."

Saint had his map in his lap. "I've seemed to have lost my way, and I can't make sense of this thing. I'm trying to get here to my hotel." He pointed at a location on the map.

The officer bent down to get a better look. That's when Saint grabbed him by the collar and yanked, causing the officer's head to bounce off the edge of the car's roof. He stumbled backwards, falling on his butt. Saint was out of the car and over the dazed officer before he had a chance to react. Saint punched him twice in the face, knocking him out cold. The chance of anyone driving by any time soon was highly unlikely, but he acted fast. He hoisted the officer up and slid him in the backseat of his rental. He quickly undressed him and then cuffed his hands in front of him.

After taking the officer's clothes, keys, and gun, he ran to the SUV. Quickly rummaging through the truck's cargo area, he found a pair of binoculars, a cigarette lighter, a roll of duct tape, flares, a canister of gasoline, and some rope. Up front, he found a pump shotgun, a bulletproof vest lying in the passenger seat, and boxes of ammo in the glove compartment for the shotgun and the Glock he'd taken from the policeman. He ran back to his car and tossed a walkie-talkie into the backseat with the unconscious cop. He then got back into the officer's truck and sped off.

Marion's estate was tucked away in northeastern La Gomera. Its landscape was dotted with palm trees, banana plants, and prickly pear cactuses. He studied the estate from the SUV while listening to the weather scanner and police radio. A news bulletin came over the radio urging residents to stay indoors and to have candles ready. The winds were nearly bending trees in half as they swayed and rocked. The rain fell in buckets, soaking everything. Saint cocked his head as he listened to the police band. The officer who he knocked out was radioing the station for help. In his Spanish tongue, the officer rapidly told the dispatch officer what happened.

Okay, Saint thought to himself. *In approximately two minutes someone from the station is going to call you, Marion. The minute you landed in LA Gomera, I knew you called your contacts at the police station and told them to give you a heads up on anything that happens out of the ordinary. I think an officer getting jacked qualifies as being out of the ordinary.*

Saint closed his eyes as he felt his body starting to tingle. *Showtime!*

"How's Glenn holding up?" Olivia asked Grace.

Both women were sitting in the front row, center seats.

"He'll be fine. You know he gets all schizo right before a show. He'll be fine once he takes the stage."

Two burly men approached Grace and Olivia from each end and sat next to them.

"Umm, excuse me, but these seats are reserved," Grace said.

"Sorry, ma'am. Mr. Seeger has instructed us to sit here."

"What for?" Olivia asked with an attitude.

"We just do as we're told, ma'am," the man sitting next to Olivia said.

She felt a chill run down her spine. She sensed something wasn't right. Saint popped into her mind. Was he all right? Where was he right now? Is what he had to do have something to do with these two goons sitting next to them? She didn't know why, but she turned around and caught a man quickly averting his gaze from her. He covered his mouth with his hand and began talking to a gentleman sitting next to him. Olivia's heart started to race.

Glenn must've let Josephine's number ring fifty times before he began banging his head against the wall. *God, this can't be happening.* He started pacing while trying to think what Saint would do in a situation like this. He peeked from behind the curtain and his chin nearly hit the floor when he saw the two men sitting on either side of Grace and Olivia. *Think, think, think. What would Saint do?* He ducked back behind the curtain and hit speed dial.

"Hello."

"Olivia," Glenn yelled into the phone. "Don't say a word. Just listen."

"It's him!" Marion screamed into the phone.

The police chief called him the moment his deputy told him about the call that came over the radio.

"Calm down, Marion," the chief said. "I'm going to send a car over—"

"No! Don't send anyone over. Wait a minute. I need you to do something for me." Marion smiled, believing he knew Saint's plan.

"Bobby," the police chief's voice sounded over the radio.

"I'm here, boss."

"I need you to go to the Claude estate."

"Roger that."

"How quick can you get there?"

"In this storm, thirty minutes."

"Radio in when you get there."

"Roger that."

The chief spoke into the phone's receiver. "Marion, are you there?"

"Yes. Excellent. I owe you one."

"Now, you know that no one is coming, right?"

"Someone *is* coming. Just make sure you call that deputy on his cell phone and tell him to stay far away from here."

"I don't want a war breaking out on my island, Marion."

"Don't worry. It'll all be over in the morning."

Saint heard the conversation between the chief and the deputy over the radio. The officer said he would be there in thirty minutes. That gave him twenty to prepare.

"He took the cop's uniform and his truck," Marion said to Jean, as he paced back and forth in his study. "You see what he's trying to do, right?"

"He won't get ten yards within our perimeter," Marion's new head of security, Roberts, said.

"I agree," Jean chimed in.

"The chief of police assured me that none of his men are coming here. So, as soon as he drives up to the gates, open fire."

"You don't think he's just going to drive right up to the gates and expect us to let him in, do you?"

"I have to expect everything from him. Just do as I say. You see a cop, shoot him. If you see that yellow police vehicle, riddle it with bullet holes. We have plenty of ammo."

"Yes, sir," Roberts said, leaving the study.

Saint drove down into the muddy valley and parked the SUV two hundred yards away from the estate. He parked it where it couldn't easily be seen. Then he jumped out and got to work.

It would only be a matter of time before the rain eased up and the truck would be spotted.

"What's up with these dudes crowding us?" Olivia said into the phone.

"Who's that?" Grace asked.

"Olivia! Please, just listen. I couldn't call Grace. She would've freaked out."

"You're freaking me out."

"Who is that?" Grace asked again. Olivia waved her off.

"The men who are sitting next to you and Grace are Mr. Seeger's men."

"What's going on?"

"There are some men in the building…Marion's men."

Olivia turned around and stared at the man who she caught looking at her earlier. This time, he didn't avert his gaze. Olivia turned back around.

"I need you to remain calm, and most importantly, keep Grace calm."

"Does this have something to do with S—"

"Don't say his name!"

Glenn told Olivia everything that was currently going on. She listened without looking at Grace, afraid that her facial expression would make Grace panic.

"Just remember what I said. Stay calm and don't leave your seats for any reason."

Olivia started to say something, but Glenn hung up. She looked at the man sitting next to her and noticed that while his arms were folded on his chest, his right hand was inside his jacket. She imagined it wrapped around the butt of a gun hanging from a shoulder holster.

"Who was on the phone?" Grace asked, getting irritated.

"Nobody."

"Nobody? You did a whole lot of talking to a nobody." Grace folded her arms. "Fine. If you don't want to tell me who he is, that's your prerogative."

"He?"

"The one you've been seeing on the low. I didn't want to press the issue when I walked in that morning and saw you knocked out on the couch in your office. I just figured you needed time to tell me."

"There is no *he*."

Grace's eyes lit up. "It's Clayton, isn't it? He came back."

"No, he didn't. And keep your voice down."

Grace looked at the man sitting next to her. "Check this out. I don't care what Mr. Seeger told you, but y'all are going to have to find someplace else to sit."

"Ma'am—"

"Ma'am, my ass," Grace said, standing up. "You and your friend need to step off before it gets real ugly up in here."

Olivia turned around and saw the two men stand up.

"Grace, sit down and leave them alone."

"What? Whose side are you on?"

"Grace, please, just sit down and let's enjoy the show. The last thing Glenn needs is to see you causing a scene."

Grace rolled her eyes at both men and plopped down in her seat. Olivia folded her hands together to keep them from shaking. When she turned around, she saw that the two men had sat back down. Just as Olivia started to calm down, Grace jumped back up.

"Where are you going?"

"To the bathroom."

"Wait! Do you have to go now?"

"Yes, I have to go now."

The man sitting next to Grace stood up.

"I know you're not going to follow me to the bathroom."

Olivia turned around and saw the two men stand back up.

"C'mon," she said, standing up. "I'll go with you."

"I'm not going with these dudes following us."

"Then just sit down, please."

Grace could see the worry in Olivia's eyes and then realized something was going on that she didn't know about.

Chapter 14

"Mr. Claude," Roberts said, entering the study, "one of my men spotted the officer's truck."

Marion's lips trembled involuntarily. "Wh-where?"

"It's a couple hundred yards away. He tried to conceal it with fallen branches and leaves. I sent three of my men to check it out."

"Just three? Are you out of your mind?"

"They're well-trained, with orders to shoot anything out there that moves."

"Idiot! Haven't you been listening to anything I've been telling you about this...Saint?"

"With all due respect, sir, he's just a man."

Marion, Roberts, and Jean flinched when they heard a shotgun blast. It was quickly followed by a succession of automatic fire, and then there was silence.

Marion got up in Robert's face. "I suggest you take ten of your men out with you to that truck. Take a good look at the remains of those three men you sent to their deaths, and then you tell me if he's just a man."

As instructed, Roberts took ten of his men out to where the truck was spotted.

"Jesus," he muttered.

His men formed a perimeter around the truck as he tried to piece together what happened. The truck's driver side door was open. Attached to it was a fishing line. He followed the end of it to the shotgun that was propped under the truck. He now knew how the first man's feet were blown off. The other two were laid next to the first, but he could tell they weren't killed there. He followed the blood trails where the men were obviously butchered and then dragged to the first one.

"Their weapons and ammo are gone, sir," one of Robert's men said.

"Yes, I know, but that's the least of our problems." He radioed into Stevens, his second in command, who was in the estate. "We have three men down. I repeat, three men down."

"Copy that, sir."

Marion closed his eyes and shook his head.

"Stevens," Roberts barked, "you've got five men with you. You know who they are, correct?"

"Of course."

"Good," Roberts said, as he stared at the lead man's naked corpse. "'Cause our ghost may be wearing one of our uniforms."

Marion ran his hands through his hair. "Did he say what I think he just said?"

"Don't worry, sir. Everything's fine."

Just then, the living room turned pitch black. Marion screamed when Jean screamed. Ten seconds later, the lights came back on.

"What the fuck!" Marion shouted, looking around deranged.

Jean had darted into a corner and was hugging herself as she cried. "I don't want to die, Marion."

"Neither do I, you stupid bitch." He turned to Stevens. "What's happening?"

"I don't know if it's the storm or our ghost, but the main power went out. The lights are back on, but they're dim, which means we're getting juice from the backup generators."

"It's not the storm. Tell Roberts to get his ass back in here."

"Be there in five," Roberts radioed in, looking around the dense landscape. He could feel Saint staring at him. He felt raindrops beginning to pelt the top of his cap.

"Sir," one of the men called out.

"Grab them up," he said, referring to the three men. "We're heading back in. Keep the formation tight, and—"

Roberts' eyes widened as his men lifted up one of the dead from off the ground.

"Grenade!" Roberts shouted.

Before Saint left the area, he had taken two grenades from one of the men and placed them underneath him. He pulled the pins, knowing they wouldn't go off until someone tried moving the body.

Boom!

Jean yelped at the explosion.

Marion grabbed Stevens. "What the hell was that?"

"I don't know, sir."

As soon as the two grenades went off, Saint popped up from the shallow grave he dug for himself and calmly picked off the disorientated soldiers, one by one, with the MP-5 he'd taken from the lead man earlier. He left one man alive. The one he figured to be the leader. The one who would tell him what he needed to know.

Roberts tried blinking away the cobwebs as he groggily got to his feet. He reached for his sidearm when he saw Saint running toward him. He blinked and he was gone. He wildly fired into the underbrush. The rain was falling in slabs, making it hard for him to see five feet in front of him.

"I know you're out there," he screamed.

His ears were still ringing from the grenade blasts. He winced and looked down at his right thigh. Shrapnel from the grenades were biting into his flesh. He spun around and started shooting again at shadows, tree trunks, and leaves swaying in the wind until his gun clicked. He groped at the MP-5 hanging across his chest and switched it to full-auto.

"Show yourself!" He hiccupped when he felt the blade bite into his neck.

"Careful what you wish for. It just may come true," Saint whispered against his ear. Feeling Roberts tense, he warned, "Nah, ah, I will slice through your jugular and windpipe quicker than you can blink."

Roberts relaxed, and Saint cut the shoulder strap of the MP-5.

"Drop the gun."

Roberts let the weapon fall to the muddy ground.

Saint spun him around and swept his feet from under him. His knee landed on Roberts' chest at the same time Roberts' back hit the ground. With the knife still in his right hand, Saint used his left to retrieve the officer's Glock and stick it under Roberts' chin.

"Make no mistake, you are going to die. How painful will be up to you."

Roberts nearly bit through his bottom lip as he tried looking Saint in the eye.

"How many more men are inside?"

"Two."

Saint kept the Glock jammed against Roberts' neck turned halfway around and stabbed him in his left thigh, twisting the blade.

Roberts hollered. "Kill me, you sick son-of-a-bitch!"

"How many?"

"Fuck you."

Saint put the knife to his groin.

"Six! There are six!"

"One more thing, and then it'll be over."

Stevens radioed Roberts but didn't get a response.

Marion's bottom lip started to quiver. He scuttled backwards and fell on his butt as the sudden gust of wind hurled raindrops at the windows, causing them to sound like pellets.

"Calm down, sir," Stevens said, trying to remain calm himself.

"Don't tell me to calm down!" Marion jumped when he heard a door slam. "That's him! He's in the house!" He dug into his waistband and drew his weapon, a Desert Eagle.

Steven's radio crackled. "That was one of our men. He said the wind blew the balcony door open and he slammed it shut."

"Bullshit!" Marion's hand shook as he tried pointing the gun in all directions at once. "He's in here. He took one of your uniforms. He's dressed like one of you," he said, pointing his gun at him.

"Mr. Claude," Stevens said as calmly as he could, "I'm here to protect you."

"You call this protecting me? In a matter of minutes, you went from twenty men to six."

"I'll call the other men to come in here with us."

"No! You tell them not to leave their posts. I'm shooting anyone who walks in here."

"Sir–"

"Do it!"

"All units remain in place until further notice."

"He could be any one of your men. I'm not taking any chances."

Steven's radio crackled.

"Stevens," Roberts said, coughing. "Come in, Stevens."

"I'm here, sir."

"Everyone's dead, 'cept me. I got the son-of-a-bitch pinned behind the police vehicle. Send Delta team."

"But, sir, they're the last five–"

"Send them! You stay with Claude."

"Send them," Claude yelled. "End this now!"

"They're on their way, sir."

Saint nodded at Roberts as he put the gun to his temple and pulled the trigger.

Marion ran into the study and grabbed the phone. Then he ran back into the living room, punching the numbers in like a madman.

"Kill Lemora's fiancée. And make sure you kill her in front of him."

Grace leaned over to Olivia and whispered, "You better tell me what the fuck's going on."

"That was Glenn on the phone earlier. There are two men sitting five rows behind us. One is white, and the other one's light skinned–"

Grace turned around.

"Why'd you turn around?"

"I wanted to see who you were talking about. I don't see them."

Olivia turned around. The men were gone.

"They were just sitting there a minute ago."

"Well, they're not there now."

"Something's not right." Olivia scanned the whole theatre.

"What did Glenn say on the phone, and why did he call you and not me?"

Mr. Seeger walked out onto the stage and stood behind the podium. "Good evening, ladies and gentlemen. It is my pleasure to introduce to you the man behind the hottest women's new fashion line…Mr. Glenn Lemora."

Glenn received a standing ovation as he walked onto the stage. He looked directly at Olivia and then to Grace. He then looked at both the men sitting next to them before beginning his introduction.

"Good evening—"

Gasps could be heard throughout the theatre as it went black.

"Hey, Chief," the dispatcher said. "This is the fifth call I received from the village claiming to be hearing gunshots coming from the Claude estate."

The chief massaged his temples as he let out a sigh.

"Should I send Jimmy over?"

"Anything on that rental car or the guy that assaulted Enrique and left him cuffed in the backseat?"

"We found the rental agreement in the glove compartment. It was rented to a George Wilham."

"Why would he cuff Enrique, throw him in the backseat, and leave the rental agreement in the glove compartment? It's like he wants us to know who he is."

"Or maybe he was in a rush and panicked."

The chief let the theory spin a couple laps in his head before rejecting it.

"Should I send Jimmy to see what's going on?"

"Yeah, send him over, but tell him not to do anything until I get there."

"Chief—"

"Do as I say," he said, grabbing his jacket and heading out of the station.

"Get up," Marion shouted to Jean.

She shook her head violently, refusing to move from the corner of the room she wedged herself into. She screamed when he squeezed off a shot, missing her by inches.

"Get off your ass now before I put a bullet in it."

She got to her feet, shaking like a leaf. Marion spun toward the window when he saw a lightening flash and pulled the trigger. The window shattered as he sent three bullets through it.

"Sir, you're going to have to give me that weapon," Stevens said.

"Bull-motherfucking-shit!" Marion now had the gun pointed at him.

Stevens held his hands up to show that he was no threat.

Marion turned the gun back on Jean and then threw the phone at her.

"Call Vince and tell him to start up the Hummer. I'm getting the hell out of here."

Jean dialed Vince's room.

"Radio Roberts. See what's going on out there," Marion told Stevens.

Stevens got on his radio. "Roberts—"

Stevens spun around with his MP-5 in hand. Marion spun in the same direction. The direction both men heard Steven's voice over a radio. Marion opened his mouth to say something but was quickly silenced by Steven's hand. The beam over them creaked. They looked up and fired at the same time. Jean screamed and ran back into the corner, covering her ears. Marion locked eyes with Stevens, and for the first time, he saw fear in the soldier's eyes.

"Marion," Saint's voice came over Steven's radio, "if you put your guns down, I promise not to kill you...slow."

Marion ran to the corner and grabbed Jean. He held the screaming assistant in front of him.

"Fuck you! Here's the deal. I got my men at Glenn's fashion show, and I gave them the order to kill him and his fiancée. They're as good as dead if I don't call them back in five minutes. By the way, Miss Martin is with them."

Instead of Marion's words stopping Saint in his tracks, it only enraged him. He dived through the window that Marion shot out earlier and shot Stevens in the back of the head. Before Stevens hit the ground, Saint yoked him up. Marion fired. His bullets buried themselves into Steven's vest and flesh. One, two, three, four, click. Marion's gun was empty.

Saint dropped Stevens and walked toward him and his trembling assistant. He snatched her out of his grip and threw her to the ground. She scurried behind Marion and back into the corner.

Marion fell to his knees, clasped his hands together, and bowed his head. "S-Saint, please, whatever you want I'll do it. I'll get it."

Saint took a step back when he saw the piss stain in Marion's pants getting bigger. "Why'd you try to have Josephine killed?"

"That wasn't me, I swear to you."

"Don't lie to me," Saint said, nudging the Glock against his head.

"No! I wouldn't lie. Not about that. I have no reason to kill her. Our businesses have nothing to do with one another. What would I gain?" Marion started crying. "You've got to believe me."

"Look at me."

Marion tried, but he couldn't.

"Look…at me."

He was able to hold his gaze for a full five seconds before his eyes filled with tears.

Saint stuffed the gun in his waistband. "I believe you."

Marion was shocked.

"Call your men and tell them to abort," Saint ordered, then drew his gun, spun, and aimed at the footsteps he heard approaching from the adjacent room.

Vince froze in the doorway, throwing his hands in the air.

"He's my driver," Marion said.

"Well, driver, I suggest you get into a car and drive!"

Vince took off.

"Make the call."

Marion looked on the floor for the phone. Seeing it, he hurried to grab it. He called the men at the Apollo. The longer it rang, the more ragged his breathing became.

"What's wrong?"

Marion was too scared to hear the nervousness in Saint's voice. He hung up and dialed the number again.

"He's not picking up." He backed up into Jean when Saint pointed the Glock at him. "I will pull your toenails out one by one. I will rip your fingernails off one by one. I will pry your teeth out one by one. Then I will peel the skin off of your entire body strip by strip."

"Pick up!" Marion's face was ghost white.

The only source of light in the theatre was the exit sign. Grace jumped as she felt someone grab her by the wrist.

"Baby, it's me," Glenn whispered.

He hopped down from the stage, grabbed Olivia by the hand, and stood them up. Both bodyguards stood, as well.

The one nearest to Glenn spoke. "Mr. Lemora, we should stay put until the lights come back on."

Glenn could hear Mr. Seeger speaking into the microphone, informing everyone not to panic, that the lights would be back on momentarily.

"No," Glenn said, "we're getting out of here."

The bodyguard held his hand up to protest, but Grace knocked it down.

"Don't put your hand in my face."

"Ma'am—"

"Ma'am, nothing. Back the fuck up."

The red-in-the-face bodyguard backed up, and Glenn made a beeline with both women to the exit sign.

Anticipating that they would run toward the exit sign, the men who Olivia saw before were waiting in the shadows. One of the men stepped out, stopping them in their tracks. When they turned around, both of the bodyguards who were running to keep up with them saw the man stepping out in front of them, and they started to draw their weapons. Glenn pointed behind the two men, but it was too late. The other man, hiding in the shadows, materialized behind the two bodyguards and shot them in the back. Olivia saw the gun flash but didn't hear the sounds. She thought maybe she had gone deaf, but then she saw the extended nozzle of the gun and realized the gun had a silencer on it.

These men are going to kill us just like the two bodyguards, and no one's going to hear us die, she screamed silently in her mind.

The man from the rear kept walking until he got into striking distance and hit Glenn over the head with the butt of his gun. Grace started to attack the man but was quickly silenced when he stuck his gun against her cheek. The man in front grabbed Olivia by her hair and forced her to her knees. Glenn started crawling toward the man who had his gun against Grace's cheek, but he stopped when the gunman cocked the hammer.

"Please...don't do this," Glenn cried.

The man smiled as he turned away from Glenn and decided to pull the trigger, but something distracted him from doing so.

Both men turned their guns in the same direction. At first, Glenn, Grace, or Olivia didn't hear it, but then the sound pounded in their ears. It was the click-clack of heels. The men froze when they saw her.

"You know who I am, no?" Josephine asked.

Both men nodded.

"Yet, you still point your guns at me?"

Both men dropped their guns to their sides like scolded school children.

Josephine was dressed in black, and her mood was blacker. She removed her shades and shoved them into the pocket of her leather trench coat. Her hand was slow going in, but it came out in a blur. When both men realized she had a gun in it, she had already squeezed off two shots. They both dropped to the floor with tiny holes in the center of their heads. Glenn hugged Grace as she started to cry. Olivia stood up and locked eyes with Josephine to keep from looking down at the corpses in front of her and passing out.

Glenn stepped in front of Grace and Olivia as Josephine approached them.

"If I wanted you dead, I wouldn't have butted in."

"What's going on, Josephine?"

"Glenn, Glenn, still slow on the draw I see."

"You know this woman?" Grace asked.

When Glenn didn't respond, she studied Josephine and remembered seeing her before.

"You! You're the woman who walked into the salon a while back." Grace looked at Olivia. "This is the woman you took into your office. Olivia, please tell me what's going on?"

Josephine pointed her gun at the gunman at her feet and fired two shots into his chest. Grace and Olivia jumped.

"He moved. I shot. Reflexes."

But, then, she realized he hadn't moved. Something in his pants moved, vibrated. She dug into his pants pocket and pulled out his cell phone. She cleared her throat and answered it with the best man voice she could muster.

"Yeah."

"Where the fuck have you been? I've been trying to reach you!" Marion said. "Did you take care of that yet?"

"They tried, but they failed," Josephine said in her own voice.

"Josephine! What are you doing there?"

Saint snatched the phone from him. "Josephine?"

"This is becoming a habit, me saving those closest to you from harm. Are you okay?"

"I'm fine."

"Don't worry they're safe."

"How did you know they were in danger?" Saint asked.

"Glenn called me."

"Glenn—"

"I'd love to chat with you longer, my love, but we're standing in the middle of four bodies. Just come back to me in one piece."

She hung up before he could say another word.

He dropped the phone. If Marion didn't try to kill Josephine, then who did? He did a mental lineup of the usual suspects and then the unusual ones. Marion's sniffling brought him back to the matter at hand. He looked down at him and raised the Glock.

"W-wait! You said you believed me."

"I do, but I don't like you."

Jean screamed as Marion's hot blood splattered her. She looked up at Saint. Blood from the hole he put in Steven's head soaked the front of his vest when he was using him as a shield. She stuck her head between her knees when Saint flinched at her. She peeked from behind her hands to plead for her life, but the boogeyman she would forever have nightmares of had vanished.

"We must get out of here," Josephine said, putting her gun away.

"And go where?" Glenn asked.

"I don't care where you go." Josephine banged the exit door open and walked into the night.

"Hold on," Olivia said, following her outside. "You can't just leave us."

"Watch me." She pulled out the key to her Burgundy S-Class.

"Josephine, wait," Glenn said, running behind her. "Is anyone else going to try and come after us?"

"I don't know and I don't care."

"Then why did you stop Marion's men from killing us?" Grace asked.

"Those weren't Marion's men. They were mine."

Chapter 15

"They were your men? I don't understand," Olivia said.

"I'm beginning to." Josephine pressed the button on her keypad to unlock the car door of the burgundy Mercedes.

"What are we supposed to do?" Glenn asked. "Four men are dead and people are going to realize we're missing."

"Don't worry about the bodies. They're gone by now."

"Bodies don't just disappear," Grace said.

"In my world, they do."

"You can't just leave us," Olivia repeated.

"Watch me," Josephine replied again as she opened her car door.

Olivia grabbed the door handle. "What if someone comes after us again?"

"That's not my problem."

"What just happened back there wasn't your problem, yet you got involved."

"Maybe I shouldn't have."

"But you did. Why?"

Josephine was the first to hear the two black SUVs gunning down the street. The first one skidded in front of the Mercedes, while the other stopped inches from the back bumper. Van got out of the first one, with gun in hand.

"Don't," he said to Josephine as she drew her gun.

"You won't dare shoot me," she said.

"Don't tempt me. Toss the gun into the car."

"I toss it, you'll probably kill us."

"You don't toss it, I will definitely kill you."

Olivia put her hand on Josephine's shoulder, indicating that she should do as Van said. Josephine bared her teeth at him as she tossed the gun into her car.

"Now close the car door and all of you walk toward me."

As instructed, Josephine closed the car door and they all walked toward him. Two men from the rear SUV got out and escorted them to the truck.

"Olivia!" Baby called out from across the street. Her and Miki had just gotten out of a cab and were heading for the theatre when they saw them getting into the SUV. Both women grabbed each other when Van pointed his gun at them.

"Come here," he said, waving them over.

Miki shook her head.

"Run!" Olivia yelled to them.

"Run and I'll kill her and dump her body right here in the street," he said, jabbing his gun in Olivia's side.

As they inched toward him, Van lowered his gun to his side. People were already stopping to take notice at what was going on. When Miki got within arm's reach, Van grabbed her by the elbow. He ushered Baby and Miki into the back of the first truck, then climbed into the back with them.

"Drive." Van pulled out his cell phone and made a call. "It's me. Take down this address." He read off the numbers to the mansion in the Catskills. "Be there tomorrow by three o'clock."

"How am I supposed to get these four bodies out of the theatre?" Seeger asked.

"I don't care how you do it. Just do it. And be at the address I gave you." He hung up and directed his attention to Baby and Miki.

"What's going on?" Baby asked.

"Right now, nothing. And as long as you two behave, it will stay that way."

Four hours later, they arrived at the mansion. Van instructed one of his men to take Baby and Miki to the master bedroom and cuff them to the bedposts. He instructed another to take Glenn and Grace to the last bedroom down the hall and cuff them to the bed. He elected himself to stay with Josephine and Olivia in the living room. His last man he ordered to lock all the doors and windows.

"What now?" Olivia asked.

Van grabbed the remote and turned on the TV. "Now we wait for Saint to call."

"And when will that be?"

"Your guess is as good as mine."

"It was you," Josephine sneered. "You were the one who gave the CIA Saint's Clayton Andrews identity."

"And once again, he was able to slip right through their hands and fall off the face of the earth."

"Germany, the assassination attempt—"

"I only wanted you wounded. I knew you would think Marion was behind it. And I knew you would bring Saint out of hiding to take care of him personally. In a few hours, we'll see if the infamous Saint is still standing. And if so, we'll see if he's still standing after I get through with him."

"Don't flatter yourself. You're nowhere near his league," Josephine said.

"I beg to differ, my love."

"Many have tried to kill him and failed. What makes you think you'll succeed?"

"I will succeed because I'm not going to kill him. What I'm going to do is far worse."

"You're a dead man. You and everyone who's down with this insane plan," Josephine threatened.

Van stood up, looked around the living room, and whistled.

"This place is beautiful. I can see why you and Saint decided to come here for summer vacations. It's a shame your last memories of this place aren't just as beautiful."

Josephine started to say something, but then changed her mind.

"I'm surprised the Ukrainian hit men got within a hundred yards of this place. Then again, you two were on vacation, so I guess that also means letting your guard down."

"Shut up," Josephine said coldly.

"They beat you for over an hour, but you didn't crack. You didn't tell them where they could find your precious Saint. Instead of killing you, they decided to let you live to tell Saint who brutally assaulted you. They would no longer have to look for him because he would now be looking for them. And looking for them he did." He looked at Olivia. "You would be in shock if I told you what your boyfriend did to those men."

"Nothing shocks me with him anymore."

"Don't be so quick to say nothing. I forgot to mention that Josephine was two months pregnant at the time."

Josephine shot off the couch and attacked him. He grabbed her arms and forced her back onto the couch.

"You bastard! Get off of me!"

Van backed away. Josephine sat on the couch huffing and burning him with a stare of pure hatred.

"But keep that little secret between us," Van said to Olivia. "Saint doesn't know that he was almost a daddy." He looked at Josephine. "You should've told them where to find him. Instead of having a miscarriage, you would've had a baby."

"I'm going to beg Saint not to kill you," Josephine said through tight lips. "Not until I shatter every bone in your body with a sledgehammer."

"That pain would come nowhere close to the heartache you've put me through for the past three years. No matter what I did for you, you could never stop talking about him. How much you miss him, how much you love him, what you would sacrifice for him, and when you found out he's banging this chick, now you wanted to kill him. Which of course I didn't have a problem with, because then, I would be the only man in your life. But, then, you had to go and fuck it up by having the nerve to want me to be your 'new' Saint. You even started calling me Saint. That's where I drew the line. Fuck you and fuck Saint! He's not all that. Anybody can point a gun and shoot. Ain't that right, barbershop girl?"

"Fuck you," Olivia said.

"Fuck me? How about a chance to kill me?" Van pulled the .45 out of his waist and dropped it on the couch next to her, then backed away.

Olivia quickly picked it up and pulled the trigger. When it didn't go off, she fumbled with the safety, switching it in the opposite direction, and pulled the trigger again.

"See, even a barber is capable of pointing a gun and pulling the trigger." He snatched the gun from her and pulled the slide back, injecting a bullet into the chamber. He looked at his watch and then sat on the couch across the room. "Y'all might as well get comfortable. Looks like he's not going to be calling tonight."

The following afternoon, Van looked at his watch and hopped off the couch. He grabbed Josephine's satellite phone and tossed it to her.

"Call him."

"He won't answer."

"Humor me."

"Humor yourself," she said, throwing the phone at him.

He caught it as it bounced off his chest. As he lifted his hand to slap her, one of his men stepped into the living room.

"Seeger's here."

"Show him in." Van smoothed out his pants and put on his suit jacket to conceal the gun in his waistband.

Seeger walked in with a nervous look on his face. "This isn't what we agreed to."

"Things changed, so I had to toss plan A out the window."

"What plan are we going with now?"

"Duh...plan B?"

"And what's plan B?"

"Before I tell you, I have to know if you're still willing to follow this through to the end."

Seeger looked at Josephine. "What was wrong with the original plan?"

"Well, first off," Van said, "she was in charge, but that was one of the things that changed, and second, I'm going to need you to play a bigger part."

"What? I don't understand. Josephine, what's going on? I thought we had a deal."

"Hey," Van said, pulling the .45 out his waistband. "Look at me. What part of I'm-in-charge don't you understand? Things are still running smooth. In fact, I'm offering you a bigger piece of the pie. So are you in or are you out?"

"Give me a minute to think about this."

"Take two," Van said, tapping the gun on his thigh.

Seeger looked at Olivia, and after a few moments, he sighed.

"In or out?" Van asked.

"I'm out."

Van winced. "Wrong answer." He raised his gun and shot Seeger between the eyes.

Olivia yelped as Seeger fell backwards and hit the floor with a thud.

"You've lost your mind," Josephine said.

"No, I lost my patience."

The bodyguard that let Seeger in stepped into the living room.

"Get Seth, and you two put him in the basement."

Olivia shuddered as the two men picked Seeger up and carried him off.

"I want to see my friends," Olivia voiced, almost demanded.

"They're fine."

"I want to see for myself."

"I said they're fine, so just relax."

Josephine stood up.

"What's up?" Van asked.

Josephine slowly walked toward him. She ran her hand down the side of his face. He closed his eyes, relishing the contact.

"Listen to me, Van, please. With Marion dead, this opens up a window of opportunity for us. Think of the countries he did business with, the clients, the connections, the money, the power."

"I have and I want it all." He inhaled Josephine's scent off the palm of her hand, and with his eyes still closed, he kissed it.

With practiced precision, she punched him in the throat with her free hand and took a step back.

Van's eyes popped open as he grabbed his throat and started gagging. He forgot how much pain he was in when he saw Josephine reaching under her dress. He fumbled at his waistband and pulled his gun. At the same time, Josephine retrieved the .25 automatic from her thigh holster. Both had their guns pointed at one another.

"Josephine, don't make me do this. Give me that gun," Van said through watery eyes.

"Drop yours and we can talk."

Van chuckled. "I think that would be a bad move on my part."

"The bad move on your part was not checking me for a weapon."

"And you just want to talk?"

"Yeah, just talk," Josephine said, her eyes turning beady.

He began lowering his gun, but what he was really doing was turning his body to the side to make himself less of a target. He sprang at her with lightening speed. She got off a shot before he tackled her to the ground.

Olivia flew off the couch and charged at Van. He wrenched the .25 from Josephine's grip and quickly got back to his feet. He brought the butt of his gun down on Olivia's forehead, dazing her long enough to shove her to the floor next to Josephine.

He stumbled back from them and looked at his left shoulder. Removing his jacket, he inspected the gunshot. The bullet grazed him. No harm done.

"Just talk, huh?"

"You came at me," Josephine said, attempting to get off the floor.

He kicked her back down. "Stay down there. I like you better there. And you..."

He slapped the taste out of Olivia. He was about to kick her, when the satellite phone rang. Everybody froze and looked at it for a couple seconds. Van finally walked over to the coffee table and answered it.

"Congratulations on another successful hit."

"Put Josephine on," Saint said.

"There's been a change in plans."

"Put Josephine on the phone."

Van walked over to Olivia, grabbed her by the hair, and yanked until she screamed.

"You son-of-a-bitch. If you hurt her—"

"What I do to her is entirely up to you."

"Where's Josephine?"

"She's here admiring the hardwood floors."

"I told her not to trust you."

"And I told her to stop loving you, but as we both know, she's a hardheaded bitch."

"What do you want?"

"I want to know where you are."

"Africa."

"You're so predictable. I figured you would go there after the job. Here's the deal. Do as I say, and I'll let them all go."

"All?"

"The whole gang is here. Glenn, Grace, and two of the women who work at the shop with your precious Olivia."

"You're supposed to be a professional."

"Which is why I'm giving you a chance to do the right thing."

"And what is the right thing?"

"You're a murderer. Killing people is against the law. I want you to go to the American Embassy and turn yourself in. Tell them who you really are."

"You know I'm not going to do that."

"Not even to save your precious Olivia?"

Saint got quiet for a moment. "How do I know you won't kill them after I turn myself in?"

"You don't, but you know for a fact that I will if you don't."

"How will you know that I turned myself in?"

"Like I said, I knew you were going to Africa. I have a man there who will confirm your arrival. Two hours." Van hung up, then got in Josephine's face. "You see my love. I don't have to kill him. Once he's in custody, he's as good as dead."

He looked at the phone as it rang in his hand. He answered it on the eighth ring.

"Is there something wrong?"

"I want to make a deal."

"A deal? Here's the deal. Do what I told you to do or everyone dies. That's the deal."

"Josephine didn't see any of this coming, did she?"

"No, she didn't."

"You've been playing me all along like a game of chess."

"Interesting analogy. I'll go with that. Josephine, Glenn, Grace, and Marion were all pawns."

"And Olivia is my queen?"

"Yes, and I believe this is the part where I get to say checkmate."

"Check, maybe, but not checkmate."

"What?"

"Checkmate means the king has no other moves."

"You have no other moves," Van responded.

"Sure I do."

"And what move would that be?"

Van shuddered as he felt the cold muzzle of Saint's 9-milimeter resting on the back of his neck.

"CHECKMATE."

Chapter 16

Josephine was the first to see Saint creep from the basement doorway. The glow on her face made Olivia turn in that direction. She opened her mouth, but he quickly silenced her by putting his finger to his lips. He was wearing a black knit hat and a pair of black overalls. Van was looking out the living room window at the scenery, oblivious to what was about to unfold.

With stealth steps, Saint crept up on him and placed the muzzle of his gun on the back of his neck.

"CHECKMATE."

Josephine and Olivia would've paid a million dollars a piece to have a snapshot of the shocked expression on Van's face.

"I've come across some pretty quick people in my time, but never one quick enough to outrun a bullet," Saint said, sensing Van was about to try something stupid.

He felt around Van's body, and finding the gun, he pulled it out of Van's waistband and put it in the pocket of his overalls.

"I thought you were in Africa?"

"I guess I'm not as predictable as you thought."

"How'd you get in? All the doors and windows are locked. I double-checked them myself."

"I stopped using doors and windows a long time ago."

"I have men with me."

"However many you have, subtract the two that carried Seeger's body down into the basement."

"That only leaves one," Josephine announced with a smug smile. "And he's upstairs with Glenn and the rest of them."

"This might sound ludicrous right now, but I was actually doing you a favor," Van told Saint.

"How so?"

"My plan was just to send you to jail for the rest of your life. She was planning on killing you."

"Won't be the first time. Isn't that right, Josephine?"

She got up from the floor and headed toward the basement.

"Where are you going?"

"I'll be right back. I'm going to go get my sledgehammer."

"No, stay put," Saint said, pulling Van's gun out his pocket and pointing it at her. "I don't trust either one of you."

"Saint," Josephine replied in a hurt tone.

"Where is everybody?"

"They're in the bedrooms upstairs," Olivia said.

"I know your man has a phone on him. Use the one you're still holding to your ear to call him, and tell him to bring everyone down here."

Van dialed Max's cell phone number. "Bring everyone down here… Just do as I say."

"Both of you go and sit on the couch," Saint said to Josephine and Olivia. "When they get to the bottom of the stairs, call them to you."

He grabbed Van by the collar and shoved him to the couch on the opposite side of the room. He sat him down and backed away from him. He kept his gun trained on him as he stood under the stairs. Ten minutes later, Max herded Baby, Glenn, Grace, and Miki down the stairs.

"Hurry up, y'all," Olivia said, beckoning them to come to her. They all ran to Olivia and hugged her.

Saint waited for Max to step down off the last stair before running up behind him and bashing him in the back of the skull with his gun.

Everyone turned when they heard him collapse to the floor.

"Saint!" Glenn called out, running to him. He hugged him and kissed him on the cheek.

"It's good to see you, too," he said, keeping his gun trained on Van. "Reach into my left pocket, take out those plastic restraints, and bound sleeping beauty before he wakes up."

"What in the hell is going on?" Baby asked Olivia.

"Girl, you don't want to know."

"Glenn, listen. Down the road about a half a mile, there's a brown Buick. I want you to take the girls out of here and head home."

"What about you?"

"Don't worry about me."

"You're not coming with us?" Olivia said.

"I got to finish up here."

Olivia looked at Josephine and then to Van. It suddenly dawned on her what he meant by finish up.

"Saint," she uttered.

"Get out of here now!"

"Look out!" Miki screamed as Seth, one of the men Saint had knocked unconscious in the basement, came flying through the doorway.

The sudden attack would have caught anyone else flat-footed, but Saint wasn't anyone else. The only thing that moved on his body was his thumb flicking on the gun's safety. He became absolutely still until the two hundred and twenty pound brawler threw a jab. That's when Saint struck with the quickness of a cobra. Throwing a left jab exposed the left side of Seth's ribcage. Saint ducked the jab, and with a right hook, he clubbed him in the ribs with the butt of his gun. Seth grunted in pain as he stumbled backward, holding his ribs. His sudden backpedal gave Saint enough room to set him up for a spinning roundhouse. The kick came high and fast. The back of his heel connected with the bottom of Seth's jaw, shattering it as the back of his head slammed against the living room wall. Without waiting to see him fall, Saint turned back to face Van, only to find him no longer in sight.

Glenn pointed toward the kitchen where Van disappeared. Saint pushed Glenn towards the women as he approached the kitchen door from the side. He flicked off the gun's safety and pushed the door open. He stole a peek inside but didn't see Van. As he filled the doorway, Van stood up from behind the counter.

Everyone in the living room screamed when they heard the shotgun blast and saw Saint lifted off his feet and hurled across the room. Van ran out of the kitchen and stood over him. He looked down at where the slug hit him and laughed.

"I should've known you'd be wearing a vest," he said, kicking him in the side.

Saint was too focused on getting air to his lungs to feel the kicks and stomps.

Van dug into Saint's pocket and took his gun back. He then picked up the gun that had fallen out of Saint's hand.

"I'm a fair man," he said before running over to Max, who was just coming back from La-La Land.

Van slapped him a couple of times to speed up the process. Once Max realized where he was, Van took the restraints off of him and gave him the guns to hold.

"If they move from that couch, shoot them."

He turned back and watched Saint struggle to get on his knees. He cracked his knuckles and rotated his head from left to right.

"I'm a fair man. So much so that I'm going to give you another chance to save your friends." He kicked Saint in the stomach, causing him to curl up in pain. "The deal is simple. Hand-to-hand combat. Kill me; you live. I kill you…they all die."

Saint looked up at him, barely able to breathe.

"Let me help you up," Van said, as he tore open the top of the overalls and started pulling at the Velcro straps of the bulletproof vest. He finally got it off and flung it. He saw the redness the size of a fist where the slug had impacted on Saint's ribs. He kicked him in the mouth, drawing blood.

"You're a fucking coward!"

Van looked at Olivia. "Is that so?"

"He can't defend himself."

Van looked down at Saint pitifully and then kicked him in the head twice, knocking him out. With a triumphant smile, he faced Olivia.

"I'm a fair man. I heard you're quite the kickboxer. Come on," he said, taunting her. "If you can hit me one time, just once, I'll stop beating on your boyfriend. What do ya say?"

When Olivia didn't respond, he turned around and started kicking Saint's limp body.

"Stop it!" Olivia took a step toward him.

Baby grabbed her arm, but she pulled away from her.

Van looked at her over his shoulder. "That's what I'm talking about." He turned to face her.

She circled him until she got near Saint, then stood in between him and Van.

"Give me a break." Van sighed and grabbed her by the front of her shirt.

Olivia kicked him in the shin and shot the palm of her hand upward, connecting with the bottom of his chin. Van bit his tongue as Olivia's blow snapped his mouth shut. She kept attacking him like an angry mama bear protecting her cub.

Van swatted her punches to the side. He feinted like he was going to throw a punch, but threw a kick to her midsection instead. Olivia folded over and fell to her knees.

Van put his hand to his mouth, wincing when he felt the huge gash on his tongue. "You stupid—" He kicked her in the ribs.

Baby, Grace, Miki, and Glenn all screamed for him to stop. Glenn attempted to run to Olivia's aid, but Max raised the gun at him and shook his head, stopping Glenn in his tracks.

"Do something," Grace screamed at Josephine, who was standing stiff as a statue.

"I am."

"And what's that?"

"Waiting."

"Waiting for what?"

Van raised his foot, intending to bring it down on Olivia's head. She put her hands out in front of her to cushion the blow. "I knew you were a lot of things," Saint said, wobbling to his feet. "But, I never took you to be a woman beater."

Van spun around and smiled. "Look who's finally awake."

Saint shook his head, clearing the cobwebs.

"I'm tired of wasting my time with you. It's time to end this," Van said.

"I agree."

Van was feeling himself so much that he never realized Saint had been carefully stringing him along up until this very moment. Van was about to learn a very important lesson. It would also be his last.

He came at Saint without caution. He threw a left jab to Saint's face, which Saint allowed to connect. He appeared to be dazed, which is why Van decided to put his all in the haymaker he threw next. He growled as he fired his right hand at Saint's nose. Saint waited for Van's fist to get an inch away from his face and then he vanished.

Van's face knotted in confusion. In his peripheral, he saw Saint standing to the side of him, watching the momentum from his punch take him off balance. In this moment of vulnerability, he turned his head and looked into Saint's eyes.

You knew I was following you that night when you went to Butta Cutz. You knew I had something to do with Josephine getting shot. And you knew I would expect you to be in Africa when you called, which is why you jumped on the first flight back to the states. All this time, you've been toying with me, playing me…like a game of chess. What I can't figure out is how did you know where to find us?

As this last question flashed through his mind, Saint smiled, making Van believe he had just read his mind. If he had gotten a chance to ask, Saint would've told him that the phone he had left Glenn behind wasn't just a phone. It was outfitted with a GPS chip. Once activated, he could track Glenn using his laptop from anywhere in the world.

Saint's smile turned to a snarl as he finished his move. He stepped behind Van and yoked him in a headlock. Without giving him time to counter, he dropped to one knee while at the same time slamming the top of Van's spine on his other knee. The impact was so brutal that Van's head snapped back, breaking his neck.

Max looked on in shock as he saw Van's neck snap. Staring at Saint like a rabid dog, he fired.

That was the moment Josephine had been waiting for. By the time he saw her, it was too late. She grabbed the vase she had been standing next to and smashed him in the face. Josephine snatched the gun out of his hand as he slid down the wall. When she got a hold of the gun, her first shot hit Saint in the forearm, the second his shoulder, and the third would have been a headshot, but the gun clicked as the empty chamber slid back.

Saint charged her as she bent down to retrieve the shotgun. He got to her as soon as she stood. They both had their hands wrapped around the gun, tussling for dear life. Saint head butted her and wrenched the gun from her. Josephine stumbled back into the wall and froze.

Saint pumped the shotgun and pointed it at her.

"Do it!" she screamed.

Saint's finger twitched against the trigger.

"You killed me a long time ago," she sobbed, "when you left me here unprotected. I don't blame them for killing our baby. I blame you!"

Saint blinked.

"I was two months pregnant with our child."

"You're lying." Saint's voice came in a whisper.

"When have I ever lied to you?"

Josephine's revelation put a halt to the adrenaline coursing through his body. The sharp pains from the gunshot wounds caused him to lower the shotgun. He bent down and snatched Van's .45 out of Max's waistband.

A thundering voice came through a bullhorn from outside.

"Attention in the house! This is Special Agent Dale of the CIA. Come out with your hands up."

Olivia started to run toward Saint. He stopped her in her tracks when he raised the .45 at her.

"Get out of here!"

"Saint—"

"All of you need to get out of here now. It *all* ends tonight."

"It's not going to end like this. I refuse for you to—"

Olivia's words were cut off when Glenn grabbed her around the waist.

"Go!" Saint said to Glenn. "They won't shoot."

It took Baby, Grace, Glenn, and Miki to restrain Olivia and carry her out of the front door. As they passed through the threshold, Olivia turned to look at Saint. His tears were falling faster than he could wipe them away. He ran toward them. Olivia held her hand out to him. He grabbed it, kissed it, and then let go. He closed the front door and locked it.

They didn't get fifty feet from the house before agents converged on them and told them to put their hands in the air. After being checked for weapons, they were escorted to a van.

Agent Dale stopped in front of Glenn. "Is he in the house?"

"Who?"

"Clayton Andrews."

"I don't know who you're talking about."

Agent Dale walked off while putting the bullhorn to his mouth.

"Mr. Andrews, I thought we had a deal."

"You're late," Saint screamed out of an upstairs window. "The party's over. Everyone's dead."

"You're not."

"That's the only way you're getting me out of this house."

"Listen to me—"

Dale ducked behind a tree as Saint emptied the .45 into the front yard. The snipers who were posted in the trees opened fire.

Dale sniffed the air and then cocked his head. "Hold your fire!" he said into the bullhorn. "You smell that?" he asked the agent who had taken cover behind a tree next to him.

"It smells like gasoline."

"What the fuck is going on?" Dale said out loud, but to no one in particular.

Then he saw it. Thick black smoke was seeping out the house.

"Shit! We need a fire truck," Dale yelled. "ASAP. And I need a couple agents willing to go in with me."

"Are you out of your mind?" one of the agents said.

"Do you know who this guy is?" Dale asked.

"I don't give a fuck who he is. I'm not trying to risk my life to catch him."

Dale looked around and realized that the other agents felt the same way. The only one who was willing to go back in was one of the women that Glenn and the rest of the women were restraining.

I can't believe I'm just going to sit here and watch this man turn to charcoal. Dale knew there was no way out. They had the whole mansion surrounded. He thought back to the call he received earlier that morning from Saint, wanting to turn himself in. He had given him the mansion's address and told him to be there no later than four o'clock on the dot or he was leaving. He looked at his watch; it was four-thirty.

Glenn stopped struggling with Olivia when the phone that Saint gave him started to ring. "Oh shit!" He fished it out of his pocket and answered it. "Hello!"

"Calm down."

"Calm down—"

"Put her on the phone."

"What's happening in there?"

"Put her on," Saint said a little firmer.

"He's on the phone," Glenn said, holding it out to Olivia. She immediately stopped struggling and snatched it from him. "Saint?"

"If we would've met in another lifetime, we would've been the perfect couple."

"Don't do this to me, please. Come out of there. I'll empty my bank account, sell my business, my house, whatever. We can disappear, go anywhere in the world, and spend the rest of our lives together."

Saint was silent for a moment, as if he was really considering her proposal.

"I'm tired of putting the lives of the ones I care about in danger. I can never love someone without someone else wanting to kill them. It'll be better for everyone this way."

"Not for me. Saint, I'm begging you. Don't leave me."

"I'll always be with you. I love you."

"Saint? Saint?" Olivia shook the phone and put it back to her ear, but all she heard was the dial tone.

Then she heard an explosion.

The house was totally engulfed in flames now, and not a single fire truck was in sight.

Chapter 17

Six months later, Glenn and Grace's dream became a reality.

"Do you, Glenn Lemora, take Grace Williams to be your lawfully wedded wife until death do you part?"

"I do."

"And do you, Grace Williams, take Glenn Lemora to be your lawfully wedded husband until death do you part?"

"I do."

"By the power vested in me, I now pronounce you husband and wife."

Everyone in the church stood and clapped as Glenn and Grace shared their first kiss as Mr. and Mrs. Lemora. Olivia couldn't wait to get out of her bridesmaid dress. She peeked over her shoulder at Baby, and by the way she kept tugging and adjusting the spaghetti straps, she could tell she couldn't wait either. She looked out into the sea of faces, astonished that the church was nearly filled to its capacity.

Toward the back of the church, she spotted a couple, an older man with a young woman. Her heart started to race as she made eye contact with him. He was thinner than she remembered, but the eyes were unmistakably his.

No matter how much we try and disguise ourselves, we can never fool the ones we love. His words echoed in her head as she stepped down from the altar. She worked her way through the crowd of guests, never taking her eyes off him. She was so focused on not letting him out of her eyesight that she bumped into Grace's grandmother.

"I'm sorry, Mrs. Williams."

"You're getting married next. I feel it in my bones."

Olivia smiled at her and then redirected her attention back to the gentleman in the back. Her breath caught in her throat when she looked up and didn't see him. Half running, half walking, she approached the young woman.

"Where did he go?"

"Excuse me?"

"The man you're with, where did he go?"

"I'm not with any man. I came alone."

"There was a man just standing next to you."

"If he was, I didn't notice him."

Olivia ran out of the church and stood at the top of the stairs looking around.

"You okay?" Miki asked, following her out of the church.

"Yeah...I'm fine. I just needed some air."

"Looks like you were looking for someone."

"I wasn't."

"You thought you saw him again, didn't you?"

Olivia sighed. "He's not dead, Miki."

"He's gone, and you have to accept that."

"That's not what my gut's telling me."

"You mean the official CIA report that Mike pulled strings to get you."

"If you count Van, his three men, Seeger, Saint, and Josephine, that's seven. But, the report says they only recovered five bodies from the fire. They identified Seeger through his dental records and the other four could not be identified. And of the four, none of them were female."

"Keep in mind, Olivia, that you have a copy of the 'official' CIA report. 'Official' meaning putting on paper *only* what people need to know. So, they could've just as easily left Saint and Josephine's bodies out of the report."

"What about the information Gates dug up for me?"

"That French private investigator you hired in France to do a trace on the name Saint gave you...Saint Mac something?"

"Saint Christopher Mackalister. Doesn't it sound like too much of a coincidence that the only Saint Christopher Mackalister he could dig up was one who died in a fire at the age of fourteen? The same age Saint was when him and Josephine left the covenant."

"Saint never mentioned the convent burning down."

"According to Gates, the fire department ruled the fire was started with rags and gasoline. Everyone was able to get out except for the young nun who was caring for the young Mackalister. He ran back in to try and save her. When the firemen tried to go in after him, a beam fell in front of them, blocking anyone from going in or coming out. You've got to see what I'm seeing here, Miki."

"Okay, for all intents and purposes, let's say him and Josephine somehow made it out of there. That still doesn't change the fact that he's not coming back."

"He came back once."

Miki looked away as she pulled her shawl over her bare shoulders.

"I know he's not coming back," Olivia finally said. "I would be able to deal with this much better if I knew for certain that he, in fact, did make it out alive and that the CIA isn't just doing one of their infamous cover-ups."

Miki put her arm around her. "There's one thing you can be certain about. You know he wouldn't want you to put your life on hold hoping that one day he will return."

"You're right."

"What you two had was special, and you will always have a piece of him with you. Right in here." Miki pointed to her heart.

They both looked up as the church door opened.

"There you are," Baby said, stepping out. "Y'all got us in here looking all over for you two."

"Girl, put your strap back on your shoulder. You ain't wearing overalls," Olivia told her.

"I can't wait to get out of this girly outfit," she said, pulling the strap back on her shoulder. "What are y'all doing out here anyway?"

"We're just getting some air," Miki said, winking at Olivia.

In Sri Lanka, in the highlands, a middle-aged woman carefully plucked the ripest leaves for her famous Ceylon tea. Long days in the sun had pleasantly baked her skin to a cinnamon complexion. She continued to carefully select her leaves, although she felt someone approaching.

"How was the wedding?" she asked without turning around.

"How'd you know it was me?"

"Woman's intuition."

Dressed in a worn, orange robe, Saint gazed over the countryside and then closed his eyes. His mind took him back to the day him and Josephine first visited the mansion in the Catskills. He wasn't too fond of the hundred-and-fifty-year-old mansion. Just as he was about to tell the real estate agent that they weren't interested, he took them down into the basement. He started explaining to them how the architect had the furnace installed away from the house so that the noise and smoke wouldn't disturb the occupants.

They stopped in front of the steam tunnel that led to the furnace. It was about five feet in diameter.

"We'll take it," Saint remembered saying. He had a contractor come in a few weeks later and re-route the steam tunnel. Instead of it ending at the furnace, it now led out into the woods to a cave.

Then his mind flashed to the moment he kissed Olivia's hand and closed the front door.

"Josephine! We've got to get out of here."

"I'm so sorry," she said, looking at his forearm. She could see the bullet protruding through the skin.

"Do you want to stay here and die, or do you want to leave?"

"What do you need me to do?"

"Follow me."

They ran to the basement where Saint had two pressurized canisters by the mouth of the steam tunnel.

"You know the drill," he said, handing her one.

They headed back upstairs. Josephine drenched the first floor with gasoline, while Saint did the same on the second.

"Mr. Andrews, I thought we had a deal," Agent Dale said.

Saint opened one of the upstairs windows and screamed out, "You're late. The party's over. Everyone's dead."

"You're not."

"That's the only way you're getting me out of this house."

"Listen to me—"

Saint pulled out the .45, aimed at the tree Dale was standing next to, and fired. When the gun was empty, he dashed downstairs.

"I'm done," Josephine said, trying hard not to inhale the fumes.

Saint grabbed her by the hand and headed toward the basement door. When they got to the doorway, he lit a book of matches and tossed it on a puddle of gasoline.

By the time Agent Dale saw the smoke, Josephine and Saint were coming out of the other end of the tunnel and into the cave. Saint moved a couple rocks and pulled out a disposable cell phone. He dialed a number and then threw the phone into the tunnel.

"What was that for?"

"I just activated the C4 I planted in the tunnel six years ago."

"Six years ago?"

"In case of a situation like this."

"Always a step ahead."

"Try three." Saint winced and grabbed the shoulder that Josephine shot him in.

Tears came to her eyes as she put her hand on top of his.

"God, I'm so sorry. Saint, please forgive me."

"Let's go!" He grabbed her by the hand and headed to the brown Buick. Twenty seconds later, the explosives went off.

"So…how was the wedding?" Josephine asked again, bringing him out of his thoughts.

"It was beautiful. It was in a big church. Grace looked stunning, and Glenn was putting a hurting on the white and lime green tux he was wearing."

"White and lime green?"

"Don't ask."

"And how did Olivia look?"

"She's the most beautiful woman I've ever laid eyes on."

Josephine put the leaves she had in her hand in the bag strapped on her shoulder and stood up. She took a step to him and ran her hand down the side of his face.

"A few months ago, I would've tried to kill you for saying that."

"What's changed?"

"Knowing that you will always love me."

"Who said I loved you?"

"Why else would you save the life of a woman who tried to kill you twice?"

"I'm still asking myself that same question."

Josephine sensed the pain in his eyes as he looked to the ground. "What is it?"

"When I was in the church, I spotted at least five CIA agents."

"That's why I was against you going to that wedding in the first place. Promise me that you won't go back to the States."

He shook his head. "I love her, Josephine."

She palmed the sides of his head and made him look her in the eyes. "Get that thought out of your mind. It can never work between you two."

Saint grabbed her by the wrists and gently pulled her hands away from his face. He kissed them and then kissed her on the forehead.

"Saint—"

He brought his lips to her ear and whispered in French, "Love has reasons that Reason can't understand."

He then kissed her once more, this time on the cheek, and strolled off into the countryside.

About the Author

Arlene Brathwaite is a mother, wife, and businesswoman. With the strength and fortitude that only a woman could have, she worked three jobs until she moved what was left of her family out of the ghetto. She has transformed her loss/pain into the will to expose the nightmares of street dreams. The nightmares hustlers seldom talk about. The nightmares that got two of the people she loved life bids in prison.

Arlene's first two books *Youngin'* and the sequel titled *Ol'Timer* were inspired by one of the many tragic events in her life that has led many teens to prison. These books were real to her in more ways than one. In the near future, she will be publishing a romance novel titled *Soul Dancing*, followed by *Devon* and an autobiography titled *I'll Take You There*. In writing these books, Arlene was able to showcase her versatility in three different genres: urban fiction, romance, and non-fiction. She believes an author shouldn't pigeonhole him/her self. Instead, they should allow their inner selves to be free to express whatever needs to come to the surface.

IN STORES NOW

978-1570876998

978-0979746208

Brathwaite Publishing
P.O. Box 38205
Albany, NY 12203
Phone: 1-(800) 476-1522
www.BrathwaitePublishing.com

Order Form

Title	Price	Quantity
Youngin' by Arlene Brathwaite	$15.00	_____
Ol 'Timer by Arlene Brathwaite	$15.00	_____
In the Cut by Arlene Brathwaite	$15.00	_____
Shipping/handling (via U.S. Media Mail)	$ 3.95	_____
	Total:	_____

Purchaser Information

Name: _____ Reg. #: _____

Address: _____

_____

City: _____ State: _____ Zip: _____

Total Number of Books Ordered: _____

We accept Credit card payments, money orders and institutional checks.
No personal checks will be accepted.

Distributors:
A & B Distributors, Inc., Afrikan World Book & Lushena Books, Inc.

www.ingramcontent.com/pod-product-compliance
Lightning Source LLC
Chambersburg PA
CBHW061953170626
46813CB00006B/2629